CRUEL PRINCE

THE SEVEN DEADLY SINACORES
BOOK THREE

AIDÈE JAIMES

Cruel Prince
The Seven Deadly Sinacores, Book 3
by Aidèe Jaimes

TRIGGER WARNING: As with many dark romances, readers should expect explicit, dubious consent scenes, as well as gore and violence.

Cover Design by: Kim Wilson at Kiwi Cover Design
Copyedited by: R.C. Craig

PROLOGUE
ARRAN

T *wo Years Ago...*

"O Lord my God, if during this day I have sinned, whether in word or deed or thought, forgive me all, for thou art good and lovest mankind. Grant me peaceful and undisturbed sleep..." Father Nikolai pauses, his palm pressed to the door of his office, and lowers his head. "O Lord, forgive me. Forgive me."

Ruslan leans in close enough so that his whispered words are audible only to the priest and me. "There is nothing to forgive when you're doing the Lord's will."

Father Nikolai lifts his milky-blue gaze to him, then looks over his shoulder at me. "Is it the Lord's will that Yegor dies or yours?"

"Both," I say. "I'm not here on behalf of your God. But I know he won't object."

"He is your God too," Nikolai says.

"He hasn't been mine for a long time, Father."

A bang against the other side of the door, followed by an expletive in Russian has the old man jumping back. "He's angry."

"Unlock the door," I order.

With a shaky hand, he inserts the key and twists. I yank him out of the way as Ruslan storms into the room, slamming into Yegor Petrov with the brute strength of an ox. The men go down onto the cobblestone floor of the church's cellar, and fists immediately make contact with flesh.

Even though they're both large and gifted with formidable physical strength, they're not matched in skill, and Ruslan quickly subdues Yegor. He pins him to the floor with a knee to his neck as he works to bind his arms behind his back.

Yegor's growls eventually die on his lips as he struggles to breathe, his face turning a deep shade of purple.

"What have I done?" Father Nikolai peers at the brawling men, his hands cupping his wrinkled cheeks.

"What you had to for your parish." I move into the room and shut the door.

It's no secret that Yegor has maintained a tight grip over his little slice of Philadelphia. Has kept his neighborhood shielded from intruders. In fact, a quick google search of Wellington Village in Northeast Philadelphia will tell you it's one of the safest places in the city to live, with low crime rates reported.

But to those who live here, who see the truth, it's hell on earth. Yegor's hold on the community, his brutal tactics and demands for the money to "keep them safe" have created an environment full of fear. If they don't pay, they lose their business or, worse, their life. If they do, they wait in terror until his next visit.

Yet the people under his thumb, the ones who hate him the most, are the very same ones who've covered his crimes. They've kept quiet about the damage to their stores, the beatings, and even the murders. All because of the fear of being too small and powerless to fight back. The question of whether they can always has them sure they can't.

It's the way of the world. Their world, that is.

In mine, however, I don't have to question whether or not I can squash a bug like Yegor. The real question is, how slowly can I do it to get the most enjoyment out of it? To really feel the thrill of ending his life in a manner befitting his low status.

Normally, I wouldn't have bothered with a piece of shit like him. But he asked for it when he took the one person who mattered more to me than my own life. One of the few human beings on the planet who deserved to be here.

So I came. I followed the stench to this old Orthodox church where he comes to confess his sins, demand absolution, then conducts his dirty business in the cellar of what he believes is a sanctuary. A place where no one would dare hurt him.

"Hand him over to me, and your parishioners will be free," I promised Father Nikolai one week ago.

"But he is Bratva" was his reply. "He is not here alone."

"Is that what he told you?" I smiled at him and gave him my number. "When he comes, call, and I will provide protection. Real protection, Reverend, at no cost to you but a phone call."

"It will cost me more than that, Arran, and you know it. It will cost me a part of my soul."

Father Nikolai may believe it's costing his soul, but he still made the call.

It didn't take much for my men to overtake Yegor's lackeys, who had no idea the priest had locked him in the lower level of the church. Now I just have to deal with their stupid leader.

Once he's secured, Ruslan drags Yegor to a nearby chair, dropping him into it like a sack of potatoes.

He's out of breath from his fight and his right eye is swelling shut rapidly. Spitting blood, he glances at me. "Arran Maxton. So nice to see you again."

"Can't say I feel the same about you."

Smirking, he tilts his chin upward. "What brings you to my lovely neck of the voods?" Though he's nearly perfected his English, he can't fully hide his Russian accent, slipping occasionally, with throaty *l*'s and extra consonants here and there.

Motioning for Ruslan to step back, I move to stand in front of Yegor. I scrutinize him and find him absolutely disgusting. "You killed my sister, so I came to kill *you*."

Laughing, he asks, "Zen what are you vaiting for?" There's no denial, his expression defiant and completely unrepentant.

Kate's beautiful face fills my mind, followed by the images of her broken body on display for everyone to see, and I'm engulfed by rage. I circle him, not to make him nervous, but to calm my own frazzled nerves and the voice in my head that's screaming for me to attack. To kill. To obliterate him.

I pause behind him and fist my hands at my sides, using the sheer power of will to keep from pummeling him. Because I don't just want *him* dead. I want anyone involved in her murder to pay the highest price.

"Who hired you for the hit?" I demand.

He turns so that his sharp profile comes into view. But even from this angle, the smile is visible. "Vat makes you think someone hired me? I'm not a hitman."

"But you are. The fact that you appointed yourself king of this town doesn't mean shit in mine. Who the fuck hired you?"

"You'll let me go if I say?" he asks in a mocking tone.

Walking to stand in front of him once again, I lean in close. "Who. The. Fuck. Was. It."

He chuckles, a crazy sort of laugh that has my jaw tensing so hard it hurts. Then he stops and looks from Ruslan to me. "You think you're so poverful, don't you? With the big, bad bodyguard to do all the vork for you. You couldn't handle a man like me yourself, you weak piece of shit!"

Abruptly, he bursts from the chair, his arms free from the rope, and attacks. Instinctively, I throw my hand out and grab him by the throat at the same time as I push all of my weight forward.

I force him back into his seat and dig my fingers into the sides of his neck. He wraps his hands around my wrist and makes a choking sound as he struggles to take in a breath, but I just squeeze harder.

I'm strong on any day, but my anger and pain make it impossible for him to pry me off.

Leaning in, my teeth grinding, I hiss, "You fucking cock-roach. Do you honestly believe he would be my partner if I was weak? The only reason he took you down was because I was afraid I'd kill you before I got you to talk."

"And because I wanted to beat up on him a little too," Ruslan says.

The veins in Yegor's temples swell and his eyes widen as

he looks behind me toward Ruslan.

"Don't look at him." I backhand him and get his attention back to me. "He's not going to help you. Who hired you?" I relax my hold on his throat enough for him to speak.

But his gaze drifts again. "Предатель." *Traitor.* "You are von of us."

Ruslan laughs. "Fucking bitch calling *me* a traitor, while *you* terrorized our people."

"Eyes on me," I say. "Who the fuck sent you? Who put a hit on my sister?!"

"I hold za answer in the palm of my hand. But you will never learn the truth." Yegor begins to laugh again in that psychotic manner, and I feel my self-control slip. My grip tightens, and my blood pressure rises with each cackle.

Unable to stand it any longer, I fully relinquish control. From the holster on my belt, I tug the Karambit knife, slice it across his neck, and jam it into his carotid artery. Blood sprays, peppering the wall with crimson droplets.

As his life spurts out of him, he drops his hold on me and just stares at me with amusement. Then his eyes are no longer on me. No longer there at all.

"Shit, you killed him," Ruslan says.

I release Yegor, letting him slump to the floor. "He wasn't going to tell me."

For a long moment, I peer at his body, my breathing hard and my heartbeat erratic. That's when something catches my attention. A business card partly in his palm, partly in his pocket, as if at the last second, before he lost consciousness, he decided to pull it out.

Taking it from him, I read the name and understand why he was laughing. He literally held the answer in the palm of his hand.

Judge Thomas Cameron.

1

SKYE

P *resent Time...*

"The investigation into the murder of Philadelphia judge Thomas Cameron is still ongoing, officials say. Cameron was found dead in the restroom of the Louda Underground Lounge; however, the search has yielded little information, except for this photograph. A man the staff identified as Hugo Sanz was seen exiting the club minutes before the body was found."

I glance at the television, my hand half stuffed into my duffel bag, and look at the blurry photograph of a man leaving the place where my father was murdered. He's dressed in a dark suit, much like what I'd expect anyone at a place like that to wear, his face angled away from the camera so that not even his profile is discernable.

"If you or anyone you know has any information on this man, please call..."

I shut it off. No one would know that man, because Hugo Sanz doesn't exist. The man in that photo is a trained killer. A professional hitman hired to take out my father. I'm convinced of it.

A revving engine somewhere in the distance has me jumping. Then when a door slams nearby, I pick up the pace, shoving clothes, jewelry I can pawn, and money into the bag.

Hurry, Skye. Move faster.

"If something happens to me," my father told Maisie and me last year. "Run. Don't stick around. Go to the house in Vermont."

I didn't have to ask why. My father had enemies. Some were behind bars, harboring a growing hatred toward the man they believed was responsible for putting them there. Never mind that they were criminals.

Others were free. Kept at bay by my father's keen ability to negotiate.

I'm not a fool. I knew he'd been blackmailed. Money and favors in exchange for his ability to remain in position. And to keep his life.

"For the greater good," he said to me the day I learned of his dealings with some of the criminals he'd sworn to protect the public from.

Yegor Petrov, the Russian gangster solely responsible for the murder of an entire family in Easton. It was my father who'd approved his release on parole a couple of years ago.

When I asked him how he justified it, he replied, "Everything needs rules and regulations to maintain order, even the streets. Yegor is one of those who enforces those rules and regulations."

"What about the police? That's their job."

He sighed and shook his head, and I couldn't tell if he

was disappointed with me for not fully accepting the idea or himself for putting it into practice. "The world is complicated and far too big for one side to rule it all. It takes the cooperation of both sides to maintain order."

My father was a good man. I have no doubt about that. A good man who played a volatile game with the enemy. Always trying to stay one step ahead yet afraid to fully win, because it could cost him not only his life, but the lives of his children as well.

Now he's dead and it's only a matter of time before the devils he made deals with come calling. Demanding their share of whatever he promised them.

I wanted time to bury him. To mourn him. But we're not being afforded even that.

Harold Greene, Daddy's best friend and confidant, told me so an hour ago. "You know Thomas made some deals. Now that he's gone, you and your sister stand to inherit a sizable life insurance benefit."

"What?" I asked in confusion. What does money matter now?

"They're going to want a piece of it, Skye," he added. "They're going to come, but it won't be enough."

"Who are you talking about?"

"Go to the house he mentioned to you. I'll meet you there in three days and tell you everything."

"Harry, who are you talking about?"

"Skye, you and your sister pack your stuff and go now. They are coming to colle—" Before he finished the sentence, he gurgled and gasped. Then a menacing voice came on the phone and laughed. That was all it took for me to hang up and finish packing my shit.

Collect. *They* are going to collect whatever money we're supposed to get. That's what he was going to say.

I don't need to know who *they* are. The malice in that laughter was enough for me to devise that *they* are not good people. And whatever debt they want to collect from me, I don't want to pay. Couldn't even if I did.

"Maze, hurry up!" I slap my palm against the doorjamb of my sister's room to emphasize the point.

"I can't find Momma's ring." She's throwing aside everything on her dresser in search of the single piece of jewelry our mother gifted her before she died.

"Maze, there's no time. We have to go."

"But the ring!" she cries, turning to look at me with huge wet eyes.

I want to take my little sister in my arms and tell her everything will be okay. That we can return and search the house when everything dies down. But I'm not sure there's time for even a single comforting pat on the back right now.

"We have to go," I say. "I'm sorry."

Hurriedly, I rush through the house and down the stairs. My heart is pounding as I dig through my father's desk, searching for the gun I know he kept. But when I don't find it quickly, I give up.

I'll have time to think later. Formulate a plan. Figure out who the enemy is. Arm myself.

For now, we need to go.

Maisie is already at the bottom of the stairs when I emerge. She's wiping fat tears from her cheeks, but her spine is straight and her chin is up. That's my girl.

"We'll be okay," I say to her and she nods. "As long as we're together, we can do anything, right?"

"Right."

Heading to the kitchen with her in tow, I peek out the door that leads to the dark back yard and to safety. All clear. Or so it seems.

The moment I open it, a man I've never seen before with auburn dreadlocks surrounding a terrifying face steps into view. "Hello, pretty girl," he sneers, displaying a row of gold teeth.

My arms go out protectively, keeping Maisie behind me as he pushes inside.

"What do—" My words are unceremoniously cut off by a spray of something wet across my face at the same time as I register a muffled crack.

The man falls forward and both Maisie and I have to jump to get out of his way before he lands on us.

"Oh my God!" Maisie screams as she looks down at the spattering of blood all over her arms.

I wipe my cheek with the back of my hand and peer at the blood smeared on it. Revulsion mixes with fear when I turn my attention to the dead man at our feet and the growing crimson puddle beneath him.

It seems like an eternity goes by as my brain pieces that information together, everything feeling like an out-of-body experience, distant and muted. The man standing at the door, a boom, him falling, and the blood. That in order for that to have happened, that means someone else is out there. Someone with a gun.

Suddenly, it all snaps into place and I snatch Maisie's wrist to pull her away from the open door. But it's too late.

A tall, well-dressed man with cold, calculating eyes fills that doorway now. He's holding a smoking gun in his gloved right hand as he steps over the body, avoiding the thick puddle of blood.

When he's all the way into the kitchen, he lifts his steel gaze to me and gives me a beautiful smile that sends a chill down my spine.

"Hello, Skye."

"Maze," I whisper over my shoulder. "Run."

Behind me, I feel her turn, but instead of escaping, she gasps and plasters herself tight against me. "Uh, Skye."

I glance back and see what has kept her in the kitchen with us. Blocking her path is a goon I hadn't even realized was there.

The behemoth grabs my sister by the shoulders and tries to pull her away. She bites at his hands while I kick at his legs. But he's too big and obviously has experience capturing people, because he's able to secure her while at the same time using one hand to shove me clear across the room.

I bounce off the counter and land in a heap on the floor.

"Calm yourself, woman," the man with the steel eyes says. "Let's talk."

Scrambling to my feet, I press myself against the wall, glancing between the armed man and the one holding my sister. Although the huge goon should terrify me more with his powerful arms and meaty fists, it's the other one who gives off an aura of deadliness that permeates the room. And it has nothing to do with the gun he's just tucked into a holster at his waist.

In the span of a few seconds, I assess the situation. Determine my chances of taking these guys on and winning. Or, at the very least, giving Maisie a chance to flee. The answer I come up with is that if I try to fight, the outcome won't be a favorable one for us.

I always appreciated my father for the extra effort he put into our education. My high GPA is something I've been incredibly proud of. Right now, however, I rather wish I excelled in combat training instead. Perhaps even self-defense. But because Momma was killed in the line of duty, he rejected the idea that either Maisie or I learn anything he considered violent. Obviously, that was a huge mistake on his part.

With useless adrenaline rushing through my veins, I begin to shake uncontrollably. "Who are you?"

The man walks around my kitchen, seeming much too large and dark a presence, while I watch him warily. Although he doesn't look like the average thug or murderer my father put behind bars, he definitely gives off a vibe that screams criminal. The powerful kind.

He pauses in front of the knife block and slides out a blade. I swallow hard as I catch the glint of the steel I've used on many occasions to slice through steaks and have the sudden vision of it slicing my throat.

"Are you going to kill us? You'll get nothing out of killing *her*." I nod toward Maisie. "She has nothing you'd want."

A chuckle escapes him. It doesn't sound like the one from the phone. It's not dramatic or evil. Actually, were this any other situation, I'd find it sexy. However, in *this* situation, it terrifies me.

Sliding the knife back into place, he angles his handsome face my way. "I don't *want* to kill either of you." He adds inflection to the word want, as if he doesn't have a choice.

"Then what *do* you want?"

"Your father made a deal with me," he informs me.

"Did you kill him for it?"

His gaze narrows almost imperceptibly, but his smile doesn't waver. "I wouldn't have killed Thomas. I needed his help. And since the life insurance you're entitled to is going into a trust until your and your sister's twenty-fifth and twentieth birthdays respectively, and you have nothing to pay his enemies with... I believe you need my help too."

"A trust?" I glance at my sister, who seems just as confused.

"Oh, didn't you know that?" He goes to the table and pulls out one of the chairs, sitting in it. When he motions to another one, I take a seat across from him. "Thomas set the five-year wait to protect both of you from anyone who would want access to it," he tells me. "But unfortunately for you, it's going to do the exact opposite because not all of his enemies have the same information that I do. They don't know you don't have money."

I stare at him, blinking. Wanting desperately to ask him if he knows exactly how many enemies we have and how much money they will hunt us down for.

"So you didn't kill our father and you're not here to kill us," I say. "Then what do you want?"

His thick brow arches and his grin widens. "I want to make you an offer you can't refuse."

2

ARRAN

I peer at the photograph of the bed my father occupied not one month ago. The warped metal frame, melted mattress, and scorched sheets were a message.

I'm nipping at your heels, it said loud and clear. *I'm close.* The two 2009 pennies left in the center on the nightstand were the signature of the man who did it. And though he usually leaves the coins over the eyes of those he kills, the fact that he left them was also a message. *Your father is already a dead man.*

How he found where I'd been keeping him, I can't be sure. No one outside of my inner circle knows of my father's struggles. Clive Maxton has an image to uphold, after all. And only a few of my most trusted men knew his location. That I'd placed him in a memory care facility after the drugs he refuses to give up began to affect his brain and caused him to need constant supervision.

But *he* knew. The man we call The Ferryman.

Some months ago, the heads of certain powerful families started turning up dead. It was Tony Sinacore, then godfather of the ruling family in New York, who made the first connection between their murders and a man named Stephen Black. That connection cost him his life.

After Luca, his younger brother, took over the *famiglia*, he called a meeting to warn those of us at risk about the new threat.

"Have you heard of The Ferryman?" he asked as we gathered around his dining room table at his home, Briar House. "He worked under Tadesco in Chicago for years, growing his power right under his nose. They called him the Ferryman because he was a smuggler. The mark he left on anyone he killed was—"

"Pennies," Noah Esposito, the new heir to the Gianni throne in New Jersey, finished for him.

Stephen eventually grew too powerful, infiltrating territories and incurring the wrath of the players he affected.

Francesco Gianni, Giuseppe Tadesco, Bryan McKenzie, Sergio Ramos, Sean Murphy, and my father. Six ruthless men, all heads of criminal organizations, came together to take him out.

Five months ago, the killings began. The men involved in Stephen's murder became targets, as did anyone who dared to replace them. All were found with 2009 pennies over their eyes, a clue as to why it was happening and who was responsible.

"If Stephen Black is dead, who's killing Dons?" Esposito asked then.

"His son," Gunn Sinclair, Luca's right-hand man, replied. "Gideon Black."

So we have a new Ferryman. A new threat. As if I didn't have to worry enough about my father accidentally killing himself, now I have to worry about an outside actor too.

Sinacore called for an alliance, appointing his wife and himself as leaders. I politely declined their government. I don't play well under someone else's authority. Besides, most of the men on that list are dead, and the Maxtons wield enough power to protect ourselves.

But something niggled at the back of my mind after the last meeting at Briar House. I'm not sure if it was Carina Sinacore's determination for revenge after her sister was killed by Gideon's assassin or the tale of the attack on Noah Esposito's loft in New Jersey, where Gideon had been set up in the building for months right under Noah's nose, that sent a chill of foreboding down my spine.

However, it wasn't until the first letter arrived at my office at the Maxton corporate office that I acted.

> *Turn him in, and I might spare you.*
> *Best regards,*
> *G. Black*

I moved my father myself, taking him to a more secure location, but kept his room in Bella Vista as a ruse.

"Join the Sinacore Alliance."

The sound of the feminine voice has me lifting my gaze from the photograph to the beautiful woman sitting across from me. "As you can see, I was able to protect my father from harm."

"And as *you* can see"—Carina Sinacore sets down a piece of paper with an address on it—"we were able to get information on him that you thought was secret. I didn't only get that photograph from the police, but I also know where you moved him."

I narrow my gaze on her. "How?"

"It was easy. All I had to do was research your family. He's at Sugar Point. The house you donated in Catherine's honor. Only, the man you gave it to died last year and he had no one. So it stood to reason that it would come back to you."

For a long while, I say nothing. It's hard to speak when you're clenching your jaw so tightly that it's difficult to pry open. It takes a lot to force the tension from my mouth and smile. "You need to work for me. I could use someone like you to sniff out my enemies."

"I'd rather work with you on getting rid of the one." She lifts her index finger.

"I don't like working for anyone. You're better off without me."

Carina returns my smile, but hers has a hint of disappointment. Her soft-brown eyes skim over my face, as if she's searching for a way in. Like I'm a puzzle she can solve, and when she does, I'll give in and join their fight.

"It's your fight too," she says as if she can read my thoughts. "We can help each other."

"How do you propose helping me?" I question curiously. "I can see how adding my technology will help get revenge for your sister. But what do *you* have to offer *me*?"

She flinches at the mention of Alma, her twin. "It's not just about the people who are dead. It's about the ones still living. If you join our alliance, we could find Clive a place that's safer. Somewhere even you haven't considered. Because Gideon is as smart as I am, maybe even more so. He will figure out where you put him."

"You couldn't keep Luca's sister safe," I remind her. "What makes you think you can do any better for my father?"

I was informed of Sofia's disappearance a week ago. Luca tried to send her to California, far from all of this. But Gideon got to her first, leaving two pennies on the counter of the bathroom she was last seen in, just like he did with my father. Which tells me she's alive. But for how long?

Sighing, Carina picks up her purse from where she set it on my desk. "Luca said you still wouldn't be ready."

"Then why come?"

She shrugs and stands, smoothing down the fabric of her white button-up shirt. "I hoped he was wrong."

"He wasn't." I stand too, a behavior engraved so heavily into my skull as a child, I do it automatically. *Stand for a lady.*

"In time, I believe you'll discover we're stronger if we pool our resources," Carina says. "Gideon is out there, plotting. And he's not going away anytime soon."

"When I make that discovery, you'll be the first I call."

Extending her hand to shake mine, she says, "I just hope that when you do, it's not too late."

"We'll be fine."

Her lips pull into a straight line, but she nods. "It was good to see you, Arran."

"And you, Carina. Come back anytime."

————

An hour after my meeting with Carina, and I'm already devising a new plan for where I can move my father. It may have angered me that she figured it out. But it also shook me. If she was able to, so can Gideon.

Father might not be happy to hear it. Or perhaps he won't give a fuck. It's possible he'll sink further into his head, into whatever world he's created there.

I'm peering at my laptop, searching for options, when a knock at my door gets my attention. "Yes?"

Devon, my assistant, enters. "Mr. Ritter is here to see you."

I groan. "Tell him to make an appointment."

"He did. It's now."

My jaw clenches. "I didn't see his name on the calendar."

"That's because I just added it this morning," he tells me. "I did ask you first, remember?"

Pinching the bridge of my nose, I lean back in my chair. "Unfortunately. Does he look happy?"

"Unfortunately," Devon echoes my reply.

"That means he has some stupid proposition to make me." I let out a long, tired breath. "Let him—"

Before I can finish my sentence, Wes pushes past Devon, almost knocking the slender man down in the process. But Devon is able to catch himself on the door.

Glaring daggers at the much beefier Wes, he smooths his hair and straightens his suit as he leaves.

If Wes noticed Devon at all, he doesn't show it. It's not like him to be aware of anyone around him. "Arran, my man. How are you?" Leaning heavily on his black cane, he makes his way to the chair across from me and sits. He's grinning like a fool as he reaches over the desk to shake my hand.

"What can I do for you?" I ask him, hoping he'll get to the point.

If possible, his oily smile only grows wider. "What? You're not going to ask me how I am? What I've been up to?"

"You only come around when you want something, so no. Just tell me what you need."

His brows arch comically. "Fuck, you really are a son of a bitch, you know that?"

"Wesley, get to the point."

"I've recently come into possession of something I believe will interest you." He places his cane between his legs and rests both hands on the handle, a large gold ring glinting from his middle finger. My gaze goes to it immediately.

The ring, with an *M* and an *H* engraved on the top and a ruby set in the center of them, is a key to the Maxton Pierce Auction House. Only the most wealthy, powerful, connected, and corrupt have access to my black-market auctions. Art, antiques, stolen artifacts believed lost long ago. You can get that and more. For the right price.

Although Wesley Ritter isn't among the wealthiest, he has connections to them, which makes him powerful. That's why he's wearing that ring, why I accepted to see him this morning, and why, when he says he has something that will interest me, I listen.

"What it is?" I ask.

"It's not a what," he says, hitting the *t* especially hard. "Rather, a who. A girl. I want to add her to tonight's catalogue at Asta."

"You know the process, Wes. I don't handle that. Ruslan does."

"I ran it by him. He also agreed you should get first dibs." From the inside pocket of his coat, he pulls out a folded stack of papers and tosses them on the desk in front of me.

"What's this?" I ask, narrowing my gaze on them.

"It's the girl's contract."

Something about the way he says it raises a red flag. I take the contract and unfold it. My eyes widen as I begin to read. "This is an indenture."

He grins. "She's my servant. Whoever gets her gets the

real deal for five years. Not that pretend shit you normally like to do there."

I look at him. "We don't force anyone onto Asta's stage. If you're selling her against her will—"

"She signed the damned thing!" he says exasperatedly. "She'll be there of her own free will to do whatever the fuck her..." he trails off, his stare going to the side as if he's trying to figure out a word. "Handler," he finally says. "She agreed to do whatever her handler wants from her in exchange for something she wanted."

"Handler." I smirk. "You mean master." I study him, wondering what exactly he's playing at. "If she's willing to do whatever you want, why sell her? Fuck her. Get your jollies and let her go."

"Because of who she is." He taps the contract with the tip of his cane. "I'll be able to make more money selling her indenture. I can get enough to buy pussy to last me the rest of my life."

"Not interested."

Yes, I own Asta. It's part of the Maxton underground empire, after all. The true source of our wealth. The Maxton Pierce Auction House sells art and antiques. Asta sells men and women to the highest bidder for their carnal pleasure.

They're not slaves. These men and women are there because they choose to be. They have signed contracts with stipulations their "consignor" must follow, clauses that give them an out if needed. But if they break that contract, they stand to lose a great deal of money.

It's nothing more than a game for most of them. A sexual fantasy both they and the bidders want to fulfill. One person to own. The other to be owned.

Sometimes, it's all about the money. And there's a lot of

it to be made with sex. I suppose one could call them prostitutes. But they are so much more than that.

Only the best is offered on that stage. The rarest finds for the most demanding of tastes. Although women will grace us with their presence on occasion, it's usually men who sit on the red tufted chairs, raising their paddles as the auctioneer calls out the obscene dollar amounts they're willing to pay.

Not me. I've never been interested in role playing. Only in getting richer.

Wes arches a bushy brow. "I think you'll change your mind when you read the name on that contract."

I drop my gaze back to the document, to the very last line, and nearly stop breathing.

Imogen Skye Cameron.

"What the fuck is this?" Straightening, I look at him. "Is this a sick joke?"

Wes laughs and lifts his hands. "No joke, I swear."

"How the fuck did you get this?" I demand.

"I told you. She got something she wanted in return for that signature."

"What would Thomas Cameron's daughter want from you?"

"Protection," he sneers. "Her father's enemies have come knocking. They think she has money. But her daddy's life insurance doesn't come in for five years. She was smart enough to seek out a man with power."

As he's saying it, I'm reading the contract. Though it would never be taken seriously in court, it would be upheld by our laws.

This Indenture Contract by and between Wesley Ritter ("Owner") and Imogen Skye Cameron ("Trustee") The Owner of this Indenture Contract therefore agrees to provide protection from any and all forms of physical harm until the herein Trustee's twenty-fifth birthday," I read aloud, then ask him, "If you're the owner of this contract, and you're obligated to keep her from harm, why bring her to me when you know what her father did? I'm the last person who wants to keep her from harm." I toss the documents back to him. "Feed her to the wolves for all I care."

His mouth quirks up to one side. "Just thought you might be interested. But I suppose now that Cameron is dead, the hatchet has been buried with him."

"He's gone. That's all that matters."

"Well, I made my offer. Some other lucky bastard can have her." With the assistance of his cane, he pushes up, then refolds the papers and tucks them back into his coat pocket. He makes to leave but swivels back to me. "Any word on who killed Thomas, by the way? Never did hear if they caught his murderer."

With my elbow on the armrest, I rub my chin with my thumb and index finger and stare straight ahead. "I haven't heard anything about who killed him."

"Hmm. Interesting. Whoever it was must have really hated him, taking him out the way he did."

"Many people hated Thomas," I hiss. "You said so yourself, his enemies have come knocking."

"But I know of only one who'd have the balls to put the hit out on him."

I shift my gaze to him. "And who is that?"

His response is to laugh, a real belly sort of laugh that has him practically bent over at the waist as he leaves the room.

But I'm too deep in my thoughts to care about what Wes may or may not know. I'm still trying to process the thought of Thomas Cameron's daughter at Asta.

Imogen Skye with the big gray eyes and the blood of a murderer flowing through her veins.

"Fuck!" I pound a fist against the desk. "Devon!"

He peeks in through the open door. "Sir?"

"Cancel all of my appointments for the rest of the day." I grab my coat from the coatrack in the corner and slide it on. "I have important matters to tend to."

Although I rarely make an appearance at that meat market, I think tonight I'll have to make an exception.

3

SKYE

The first auction I ever went to was on my eighteenth birthday. Daddy took me so that I could find something rare and unique. Although I went to many more after, that was the one I'll always remember. The thrill and excitement of trying to outbid everyone else. The disappointment of losing a chance at the antique mother of pearl music box.

I had to settle for something within the budget he set for me, but the experience more than made up for it. It's what had me going back again and again. There was always this quiet tension in the room, where men spoke with their eyes and body language. They assessed their competition. Were they richer, bolder? How high would they be willing to go?

The auctioneer would begin his fast chant, then the paddles would go up. "I hear ten thousand, do I hear fifteen. I have fifteen, can I get twenty. Twenty thousand, can I get twenty. I hear twenty, can I get twenty-five."

And so it would go, higher and higher, and my heart

rate would increase along with the bid. Who would win the prize?

I never imagined I'd be that prize one day. That I'd be the thing that men would bid on, raising their paddles as the auctioneer performs his chant.

Hell, I never even imagined a place like this existed. Asta. An underground auction house in the heart of Philadelphia, where only the wealthy and discreet get an invite.

"Ten thousand. I hear ten thousand, can I get fifteen?" The auctioneer's voice can be heard saying through the speakers in the ceiling of the dressing room I'm in. "Fifteen thousand going once, going twice... Sold to buyer number eleven."

Someone whoops and several of the women nearby applaud. As if it's a good thing to be sold at an auction. Like a piece of cattle. Worse, a sex slave.

Although, by looking at everyone here, they're not bothered by it one bit. However, unlike most of the women here getting dressed and pampered, I'm not receiving money or pleasure out of this.

"Champagne?" an Asta staff member asks me. She offers the tray filled with champagne flutes.

I lift my hand and decline politely, only to have another server offer me little caviar sandwiches and yet another, hot wet towels. Like it's a damned spa.

"How much is your starting bid?" the very handsome and very flamboyant guy getting ready beside me asks. "I'm asking twenty for a week. And I'll do anything. It's in my contract." He turns to me and winks.

"Ten thousand," I say.

He rears back as if I said something highly offensive. "Ten thousand? Girl, you have to ask for a lot more than that. Do you know what those savages out there will want from you?"

"Everything?" I say sarcastically.

"Exactly. They don't come here for no vanilla sex. They come here cause they're kinky fucks. Mouth, ass, ropes. Some will even cut you."

"Cut me?"

Grinning, he dabs gloss over his full lips and gives himself one last glimpse in his mirror. "That one's my favorite. You'll learn yours. Next time, you come to me and I'll help you draw up that contract right."

"Caleb Waters, you're up!"

"That's me, honey. Good luck." He rushes off with excitement, and for a moment, I envy him.

Perhaps I'd be excited too if I was here for the money. But whatever amount is agreed upon, I won't see a cent of it, not until I complete the single task I was assigned. Then I will get enough money to pay off any of our enemies, and, most importantly, gain Maisie's safety.

I move to stand before one of the many mirrors placed around the room and peer at my reflection. Yes, I look beautiful. The stylist, Haley, did good with the dress she chose for me—what little there is of it, at least.

Although the silver mesh tunic covered in dozens of tiny crystals does little to hide the skin beneath, my nipples poking through the delicate material, or the darker thong I was given for a modicum of modesty, it complements my long dark hair and gray eyes.

Sparkles of light dance over the shiny stones as I move, and I'm suddenly transported to another time where I wore a silver dress. Only, that one wasn't see-through. It was a formfitting gown, tight enough to be considered sexy, but not so much that it lacked class. The perfect choice for

Mayor Hawthorne's annual Christmas gala, where Daddy walked proudly arm in arm with Maisie and me.

The girl getting me ready to be auctioned off like a prize returns from wherever it is she went. "Lift up your hair for me, gorgeous," she says, startling me because, for a split second, I'd forgotten where I was. I do as I'm told and she fastens a thin diamond choker around my neck. "There. All done."

I turn to the tall redhead beauty standing beside me. "Aren't you going to do my makeup?"

"What would I add? You already have dark lashes and pink lips. Men prefer less anyway."

Offering her a shaky smile, I nod but worry it won't be enough to entice my mark. The man I've been sent to extract a single piece of information from. Arran Maxton.

He's been described as insanely handsome, aloof, and a playboy of the worst kind. The sort who only dates blonde waiflike models, and only for a single night. I've seen him on a handful of occasions, in passing, at charity events.

What they say is true. He *is* insanely handsome—tall, wavy blond hair, and a jaw so sharp, it could probably cut diamonds. The perfect match for those models he dates.

Although he never looked our way, I'm not sure if that was because he's aloof or simply due to the fact that he's the Maxton's representative and has to carry himself like the rich, powerful man he is.

But those aren't the things that concern me. It's the accuracy in types of women he dates. All I've ever seen attached to his arm *are* blonde waiflike models and actresses. Women I don't resemble in the least.

"What if he doesn't bid on me?" I asked when I was made that offer I couldn't refuse. "I might not be his type."

"He will. There will be nothing more he'll want than to

own *you*." The emphasis was put on the word you. Not own. Which meant that it wasn't that Maxton wanted to own someone, but would want to own *me* specifically.

When I asked why, the reply came with a chuckle. "I'm sure he will tell you himself."

"You okay, honey?"

"Jesus!" I jump at the light touch on my arm and spin toward Haley. I'd completely forgotten she was standing there. "I'm sorry." I give her a smile I certainly don't feel. "It's just nerves. I've never done this before."

"Don't worry. You're very pretty. I'm sure you'll go fast. Just need one more thing." From a bag tied to her waist, she pulls out something that looks like a charm and attaches it to my choker. "There. Now we're ready."

My brows pinched together, I draw closer to the mirror. "Is this a collar?" With trembling fingers, I touch the diamonds around my neck, stopping at the tag with the number sixteen eighty-nine attached to a loop in the center.

"It's your lot number." She shrugs. "And yes, it's a collar. Everyone seems to like it."

I drop my hand to my side, wondering if this could be any more demeaning. Who would have ever thought one of the honorable Judge Cameron's daughters would be standing here half naked and wearing a collar, about to be sold to the highest bidder. It's so ridiculous, I could laugh.

"Have you ever gone on stage?" I ask Haley. "Have you worn a collar too?"

"On occasion, I do. Usually for a week at a time. That's all I'm capable of giving. Then I take a nice vacation with the money." She slides the palm of her hand down my side, smoothing out the fabric.

I follow her movements, watching as she fusses over my

dress and hair. Making me as enticing as she believes I should be. Then I lift my gaze and stare into my eyes through my reflection.

My thoughts go to Maisie, to the face so similar to mine, and I wonder what she's doing at this very moment. Is she being kept safe as promised? Is she calm? Is she suffering? Is she behaving?

Like me, she's not exactly the obedient type. It will be hard for her to keep her head down and do as she's told.

Maisie. She fought so hard against the man who held her, screaming at me when I accepted the offer to be placed at auction.

I hate that she had to watch me give in and submit. It's not the example I wanted to set. But I did it for her. For her future. So that her life wouldn't be cut short. Because fifteen years old just isn't old enough.

Twenty isn't either. The thought takes me by surprise because, until now, I saw myself as a grown woman. I might not be able to legally drink for six more months, but I can own property and vote. According to the law, I can even fuck. And yet I've barely lived.

This time, I do laugh.

"What's so funny?" Haley asks.

My laughter fades. "Nothing," I say. "Nothing at all."

She gives me a curious look. "All right. Are you ready?"

I give myself one last glance and wonder how much of me I'll see the next time I peer into a mirror. If I'll be recognizable at all.

———

Asta is much larger than I'd thought. With the in-ceiling speakers, it was easy to imagine that the auction hall itself would be right next door, when, in fact, it's actually located down a long hallway. Long enough to make me wish the strappy heels Haley paired with the dress were more comfortable. Long enough that by the time we reach the entrance to the back of the stage I'll be presented on, I'm trembling so hard that I can barely walk.

Haley opens the door and we move inside. It's dark here, like one would expect the wings of a stage in a theatre would be. Several people mill about, staff members and other girls waiting for their turn.

Beyond them, at the brightly lit podium, is the auctioneer. "Sold for ten thousand to number three," he booms as he brings down his gavel.

The pretty blonde beside him squeals with delight and waves at someone out of sight as she's escorted off the stage.

"Where are they taking her?" I whisper to Haley.

"She'll go into a waiting room until payment is made."

"What if the bidder can't afford it?"

Her face snaps to mine. "Then they've come to the wrong place," she says in a tone that answers my question more than her words do. It says they'll pay one way or another. But they do pay.

Wrapping my arms around myself, I lean forward so that I can peer into the main hall. Although the room is dim, there's enough illumination to easily view its opulence. The walls covered in dark-gray damask, huge crystal chandeliers hanging over deep-red velvet chairs and marble tables with expensive wines.

Lavish and richly sensual, this is a place that caters to a very demanding clientele. Only the best for them. And that goes for *everything* offered here.

Another girl goes up, very curvy with lovely brown skin

and nearly black eyes. The exotic beauty goes for thirty thousand. She elegantly inclines her head before she's escorted off.

"Thirty thousand," I say in astonishment. The amounts spent here are insane to me. "How much money do these people have?"

"A lot," Haley replies. "That was Anika Davi. The same man always buys her for a week."

"Why bother with this, then?"

"For the fun of it." She takes my hand.

Thirty thousand for a week? If only I'd known about this place sooner, I may have been willing to offer myself for a few weeks. Perhaps I could have made enough to pay off whatever debt is owed.

But it's too late now. At this point, it's not the money I'm here for, but as the only way to set Maisie free.

Now my only concern is that the right man bids and wins. Arran Maxton. Although with the five-year contract on top of the protection stipulation, I'll be surprised if anyone shows interest at all.

Haley takes my hand. "Come on, you're up." She tugs me closer, up two steps, then stops right before we come into view of the audience.

"Up next is lot sixteen eighty-nine," the auctioneer says.

Haley gives me a little push. "Good luck."

My heart jumps and lodges itself in my throat as I move to stand in the circle beside the auctioneer as I was instructed.

"And here we have lot sixteen eighty-nine, gentlemen, sixteen eighty-nine in the catalogue. Twenty-year-old female for a five-year transferable contract. Bid starts at ten thousand dollars. Do I have ten thousand? Can I get ten?"

As he begins his chant, I look out into the hall, scanning

the faces of the people in the audience, searching for Arran Maxton. But if he's there, I don't see him.

Everyone is peering into their large handheld devices that Haley said contain the catalogue. It feels like an eternity before anyone glances back up. Then they all seem to do so simultaneously. Going from the description of what my contract entails to me, scrutinizing me, determining if I'm worth such a commitment when all they want is fun.

Without removing their gazes from me, they whisper among themselves. I am acutely aware of the sheerness of my dress, of how it does little to conceal what's beneath. Heat creeps into my cheeks, but I fight the urge to cover myself. The whole point is to sell. To entice a buyer.

Like a whore.

Pushing away the embarrassment of this humiliation isn't difficult. All I have to do is conjure up the image of Maisie's face. To imagine her locked up in some shithole, depending on me to succeed. And knowing her, doing so with extreme impatience.

Shit. I hope she doesn't do anything stupid. Like try to rescue *me* instead.

A paddle goes up. It's an elegant woman, maybe in her early forties, in the front row, who reeks of money. And I think to myself that if it all goes to hell, it might not be so bad to end up with her as I regroup. Maybe with enough time to formulate a plan, time where there's not the barrel of a gun pointed at my head, I can get Maisie and me out of this.

The chant continues. "I have ten, can I see fifteen."

To my shock, and because I didn't know if I'd get only one bid, another paddle goes up. "I see fifteen, can I get twenty."

My heart rate increases as the bids do, blood pounding

in my ears until I can barely hear what's being said. Fifty thousand, sixty, eighty, one hundred, the amounts rise fast. But just like my indecent attire doesn't matter, neither do the bids. All that matters is that the one man I need to make a bid isn't even within my sight.

Oh my God. What if he's not here? What if I'm sold to the wrong person? What if I did all this for nothing and I end up losing Maisie?

"One hundred and fifty thousand, can I get one fifty. Look at how pretty she is, and don't forget, the contract *is* transferable. I want to hear a one fifty."

An old man sitting three rows back smiles. He's been watching me. Waiting. I've seen his kind many times at auctions. The one who waits till the last second, then sweeps in with a ridiculously high amount no one else wants to outbid.

His lips pull up into a salacious grin, like he can't wait to start this game he's used to playing, and my stomach sinks.

No, no, no! The words blare in my mind as he begins to lift his paddle with the number sixty on it.

"Five hundred thousand," he calls out proudly.

I look around the room almost desperately, searching for the face of the one I'm meant to go home with.

He said Arran would want *me*. *He* said with complete certainty Arran would buy me. *He* also said my and Maisie's lives depended on it.

But as the seconds tick by and the auctioneer can't get another bid—because who in their right mind wants to buy a five-year contract for more than five hundred thousand dollars—and number sixty's grin begins to widen, all seems lost.

My mind races with possible solutions. I could tell them

to stop. That this was all a huge mistake. They'd have to release me. But I'd just be thrown out to where my enemies are waiting to get their claws in me, and Maisie would die.

I could go through with this and hope for the best. But when he looks at me with those beady eyes, like he's already undressing me, I cringe at the thought.

"Five hundred thousand going once," the auctioneer says when no one else bids. "Going twice..."

"Wa—" I begin to protest but am cut off by the deep rumble of a voice far in the back.

"One million dollars."

There's an audible gasp and excited chatter erupts as the crowd collectively turns toward the sound.

"What was that?" the auctioneer asks. "Who bid?"

Suddenly, Arran Maxton is filling one of the darkened doorways, his presence instantly permeating the space. My lips part on an intake of breath as the intensity of his gaze touches me, damning and hard and laced with predatory interest.

Without taking his stare off me, he says, "I did. One million for the girl."

Number sixty huffs as he adjusts his tie, his feathers visibly ruffled. But he does nothing. Says nothing. Just spins in his seat and stares straight ahead.

"Number one bids one million," the auctioneer says. "One million going once. Going twice... Sold! To bidder number one!"

Our eyes are locked as the mallet comes down onto the wooden block, but he might as well have slammed it into my gut, because it knocks the wind out of me.

I now belong to Arran. He didn't allow anyone else to purchase my contract. Everything has happened as it should, as I was told it would, and yet I find it hard to breathe because what comes next is even more terrifying.

"Do whatever it takes to earn his trust," I was ordered. "Fuck him. Love him. Give him your fucking soul. I don't care. Find out where Arran is hiding Clive and no one will ever bother you again. Your sister and you will be free from it all. Maisie will be safe."

There it was, the offer I couldn't refuse. My sister's safety for a piece of information from a man I've never officially met before.

Only, he's not looking at me like a stranger would. He's looking at me like he knows me. Like he knows something about me. And for a second, as he disappears back into the shadowed doorway, he looks at me like he hates me already, even before I've had a chance to betray him.

I wonder, as I'm escorted off the stage, what I'm missing. But whatever it is, it's not as important as the task at hand.

Earn Arran's trust. Find out where he's hiding his father.

Then pass the information to Gideon Black.

4

SKYE

I wait for an hour in what most would consider a relaxing space, with cream tufted chairs and plush pillows and tea served in little ceramic cups, as the transfer of my ownership is completed. But the waiting itself is what has me tensing more and more by the second.

Once it's done, Wesley Ritter will then give proof of purchase to Gideon and collect his payment. As for me, I will be taken to Arran's house and pray I don't fuck up.

I'm so on edge thinking about everything that's still to come. Of how close I came to going home with someone else and what that could have meant for Maisie. Of what it means for me now that everything turned out as it should.

The fear of the unknown has me sick to my stomach.

Think of Maisie. Think of Maisie.

Only, I don't need to remind myself to think of her. That's all I do. Is she terrified? Or is she going to view this as an opportunity to play the hero, like in one of her sketches?

Please don't do anything stupid, Maze.

"You're good to go." Haley peeks her head into the room. "Mr. Maxton is waiting for you outside."

I force myself to stand on shaky legs and follow her to the exit. "That took longer than I expected."

She glances back at me. "There was a discussion over the validity of the bid since Mr. Maxton wasn't registered tonight. But he owns the place, so..." She lifts a delicate shoulder.

"Yeah, I guess that makes sense."

Haley stops and turns to me, and for the first time, I notice the cheerful disposition she had earlier is completely gone. "I've never heard of him placing a bid on a girl. Like, ever. He rarely even makes an appearance. Does he know you or something?"

I shake my head. "I've never met him before."

She scrutinizes me in a totally different way than she did before. This time, it's through the lens women use to judge possible rivals. Is she pretty enough? Skinny enough? Good enough?

I'm not sure that I measure up to her standards. But in the end, she says, "You're lucky. Congrats."

"Thanks."

I'm taken through to the rear of the building, where several men with ear mics guard a single metal door. One of them opens it for me, and beyond it, I see the large black car waiting sleekly in the night. Though I can't immediately identify the make or model, it reeks of old world money, a Rolls-Royce perhaps.

The driver, dressed in a formal uniform, is standing near the back. He opens the door as he greets me. "Miss Cameron."

I peek inside the posh leather interior as I make to enter and swallow hard when my gaze meets Arran's. Unable to help it, I pause with one leg in the car, one out. As if I have the choice to run.

"Please, come in," Arran urges, his voice deep and satu-
rated with something dark.

"Mr. Maxton," I say.

The door shuts after I slide in beside him. I glance out
the window while the driver goes around the car and gets
into the front seat.

"I hope your night has been good so far," Arran says in
that rich tone.

I give him a side-glance. "It's been all right."

"You're nervous."

"This is the first time I've ever done anything like this."

"I know." He stares ahead then, his jaw clenching and
unclenching. "Take us home, Frank."

"Yes, sir."

Fifteen minutes later, we arrive at his house off
Delancey Street, near Rittenhouse Square. Though it's not
far from my house in Chestnut Hill, it might as well be a
trillion miles away, on another planet, with how distant I
feel from my old life.

Arran steps out of the vehicle and comes to my side to
let me out. He extends his hand to me. I hesitate, staring at
it several moments before taking it, then watch as it engulfs
mine, closing around it tightly. More so than is necessary to
assist me out of the car.

It's a show of power, I realize, when I trail my gaze from
our hands to his face. He's still tense, the tic in his jaw
pulsing.

He escorts me up a set of five marble steps to the double
doors. Before we reach the top, they're opened by a man
dressed in the same attire as the guards I noticed at Asta.

"Good evening, Mr. Maxton." He inclines his head.

"Charles," Arran greets.

The man turns to me and I smile nervously. "Hello."

"This is Imogen," Arran tells him. "She'll be staying with me for a while."

Charles nods. "I will alert the rest of the staff."

We walk into a small vestibule, where two more men sit at a long desk. At the other end is another set of marble steps and an arched door. When we go through it, I realize that *this* is the actual entrance to Arran's lavish home.

When he shuts the door behind us, I say, "You have armed guards."

"My life requires it."

I take everything in as we move through the formal foyer, with its high coffered ceiling and black-and-white checkered floors. As we pass by the wide openings that lead into the library and living room and other smaller sitting areas, I get the feeling no woman lives here.

Everything is dark, heavy, and masculine. Practically every space boasts bold wood paneling paired with blue or green patterned wallpaper. Tufted leather couches and chairs are sitting on thick muted rugs, and what looks like hand-carved art collected from around the world is sporadically strewn about.

An attempt has been made to break up all the darkness by using tall palms and ferns. But it's not enough to cut the overbearing feeling of the house.

Just like the man who owns it. The man who owns me too.

He releases my hand when we enter the study at the rear of the house, and as my blood begins to flow into it, causing it to pound, I realize just how tightly he was holding it.

"Sit," he tells me, indicating a spot on the floor across from the desk.

Frowning, I question, "There?"

"Yes."

I glance at one of the chairs across from him but do as he says, tucking my dress under my knees. He wants me on the floor? Fine.

Arran goes around his desk and sits behind it, all the while his scowl staying on me. He remains like that for a long time. So long, in fact, that I begin to squirm under his scrutiny.

"You have a nice house," I say, trying to fill in the void of sound.

"Is that how you really feel about it?" he asks. "I'm very good at reading people. This house makes you uncomfortable."

"It's not the house," I blurt before I can think better of it.

He smiles. "It's me. I make you uncomfortable."

"Yes."

Bringing his fingers to his chin, he narrows his gaze on me. I focus on the large ring on his index finger, noting the way the ruby in the center glints. But it's difficult to avoid his eyes for long when I can feel them pressed to every inch of my body.

I confirm this when I look up and find them trailing over me. It's not in the same salacious way the men at Asta did. But it's still a hungry stare. There's desire in it I don't believe he's even trying to hide. But there's also something else. Another emotion I see, one that speaks of restrained aggression.

"Are you afraid of me, Imogen?"

"Skye," I whisper, making sure to maintain eye contact. Needing to reassure myself that, though I *am* afraid, I'm not a coward. "I prefer to be called Skye."

"Why did you sell yourself at Asta?"

Shrugging a shoulder, I say, "Money. Like everyone else."

"No. Any other woman I would have bought would be crawling to me right now, desperate to suck my dick and earn her stay."

"Is that what I'm supposed to be doing?" Is that why he's looking at me the way he is? Because I don't know how I'm supposed to behave? Because I'll do it. I'll do whatever I have to in order to achieve my objective.

I make to move, but he lifts his hand to stop me.

"Stay where you are," he says and I flinch.

"I'm sorry. I thought—"

"For now, I just want you to sit there. Be the pretty object I purchased. Nothing more. Nothing less. Understood?"

I nod, determined to be a fucking statue if that's what he wants.

With one last glance at me, he opens his laptop and begins to work. For over an hour, he does this, a scowl painted harshly over his features. Only every once in a while does he peer over the screen at me, and when he sees me, it's very much like he's looking at a priceless object. His gaze goes over me, his brows pinched together as if he's trying to make sense of me the way one would a piece of art, then he goes back to work.

Damn Gideon for throwing me into this so unprepared. When I asked for information on Arran, for any clue on how to go about appealing to him, he said it would be better if I came in blind. I call it coming in stupid.

My back starts to hurt, but I fight to keep my spine straight. In order to distract myself from my discomfort, I study my surroundings.

Much like the rest of the house I glimpsed, this room is

all dark leather and polished wood. Old tomes line the shelves of three bookcases, with framed photographs placed here and there.

I squint in an effort to view them better, but they're too far away to be clear. However, even from this distance, I can tell they're family photos.

The Maxton family has been around for a long time. Old money that came from railroads and banking to form the largest private lending company in the States. Most everyone has heard of them because they own half the city and they're known for their charitable donations to children's hospitals and cancer centers as well.

In one of the photographs, I believe I can make out the father, Clive, with one of his previous wives. To one side is his eldest son, Landon. On the other are Arran and a much shorter woman who could be his sister, Catherine.

As I stare at the picture, my mind drifts with unanswered questions that have been nagging at me, yet I know better than to ask them. Why does Gideon want Clive? Why target Arran for the information when he could have gone after Landon or even Clive's wife? And why was he so sure I was the perfect bait for Arran?

As I think that, I turn to look at him and freeze. He's observing me again, acutely and severely, and making no attempt at hiding every emotion. Hate. Lust. Desire. Disgust.

But it's what he asks me next that answers at least one of my questions. It tells me exactly what's on his mind right now.

"Are you a virgin, Skye?

5

ARRAN

Imogen Skye Cameron. Skye.

I've never seen anything like her. I use the word *thing* because she cannot be a person to me. Not when the blood of Thomas Cameron flows through her veins.

Monstrous as she might be, I cannot deny she is utterly perfect and utterly beautiful. Utterly surreal with large gray doe eyes and a pouty mouth that instantly brings sex to mind. The exact blend that makes me hard and desperate to have her. And it makes me hate her all the more for it.

She's been sitting on the silk Persian rug I acquired two years ago at Maxton House. The stolen piece that was once kept in a museum in England came in, and I knew it had to be mine, no matter the cost.

Just like her.

I set Skye on it because in the same way I shouldn't touch her, I shouldn't touch the rug. Shouldn't even have it on display. But I have it laid out it in my most used room because I want to see it always, want to enjoy its beauty. I love knowing that something so priceless is at my feet.

And fuck me, but *she's* so much more enticing to look at

than an old rug. As much as I've attempted to concentrate on emails and approvals, my gaze inevitably goes back to her, and it lingers.

Everything about Skye screams for me to touch. To enjoy and feel her writhe beneath me. Her mouth, plump and pink, and that body the silver dress clings to, displaying lush breasts, a tiny waist, and legs for days.

She's staring hard at something on the shelves, fully displaying the length and grace of her ivory neck adorned with the diamond collar. I imagine what it would feel like between my hands as I squeezed with determination. Would she plead for her life with every last breath? Would her heartbeat increase as she fought, or would she go down easy, like a lamb?

Then my mind wanders again, and I imagine what her skin feels like there. What it would taste like. What she'd do if I squeezed only a little as I fucked her. Would that turn her on? Would it make her wet to know that her life is in my hands like that?

My dick twitches as blood rushes to it, and I damn myself for wanting to fuck her more than I want to kill her. It makes me question my reasons for buying her ludicrous contract in the first place, not that I have a solid answer for that.

After Wes left my office, I thought about what he'd said. The daughter of Thomas Cameron would be at Asta.

He'd believed I'd be interested. He'd been right.

Most of the underworld in Philadelphia has heard of the tension between the judge and the Maxtons. That he was vying for our support in his bid for Senator. But Wes knew more than that. He knew I suspected Thomas's involvement in Kate's death, and he dangled the carrot in front of my face.

After leaving the Maxton corporate office, I went to see my father. For hours, I sat by his side as he went about his daily routine—sleeping, eating, watching television. Although he's no longer abusing drugs—because he's not allowed to—he's still not all there. Because it wasn't the drugs that took him away. It was Kate's death.

Which means Thomas didn't only kill my sister. In a way, he also killed my father.

By the time I left him, I was consumed with thoughts of the past. Kate, Thomas.

Skye.

Though I was intrigued by the idea of her being sold, of Thomas's sins being so great that his daughter inherited the debt after his death, in the end I determined I'd do nothing about it. Leave her to her fate. However, I still found myself driving not home, but to Asta. I had to see for myself that it was true. I *needed* to see.

I paced the empty corridors of what I call the "meat market" until night came and brought people with it. I crept to the shadowed doorway between the reception and auction halls, watching with a sort of curiosity more than anything, wondering who would take her home.

Then she was brought on stage and her huge gray eyes lifted, and though she couldn't see me, I could see her, and the world came to a complete stop.

I'd glimpsed Skye on a few occasions. Events where she paraded next to her father, dressed in expensive designer clothes and appearing conceited like all the other rich brats. I noticed her beauty in a dispassionate sort of way. Registering her presence, but not focusing on it.

But now...

Now I realize it's not that I hadn't focused on her, but that she hadn't turned those eyes on me. Hadn't captivated me. Assaulted me. Because that's what it felt like when she looked my way, like a fucking assault on my senses. A wrench thrown into a powerful well-oiled machine, now rendered useless.

I was mind-fucked and gut-punched, and for several long moments, I was left with nothing but the ability to stare at her. To take in her messy dark waves with her disheveled bangs that let me know she'd been tugging on her hair, running her fingers through it, and I wanted to dig my fingers through it too. I watched as her pink tongue flicked over her plump lower lip, then she nervously bit it, and I wanted it to be my teeth that sunk into that flesh.

It took a lot of willpower to remind myself that she is Thomas Cameron's daughter and the only thing I should want from her is retribution. So what that she's innocent of his crimes?

I didn't know her reasons for ending up at Asta, offering herself up to the highest bidder in exchange for protection. I didn't care. Let her be sold off to anyone willing to take on that mess.

Then Peter Hunt bid, and the image of her in his bed, of him between those long legs with his hands all over her soft skin, fucking her, filled my head. I couldn't allow it. Would not allow it.

One million dollars. Not unheard of but hard to top. And even if anyone had, I would've gone higher. Because the moment she turned her gray gaze to me, I knew there was no way in hell I'd let anyone else have her. Not Peter Hunt or any other fucker. Ever.

Now she's mine to do with as I wish. And I wish for so very much from her. I want it all and in every way.

I shift and she turns to me, our eyes locking. Her lips

part in a silent gasp as if she can read my thoughts, see what I've just seen in my head.

"Are you a virgin?" I ask her, hoping she'll say no, because it would make every obscene thought of what I'd like to do to her seem less brutal. Hoping she'll say yes, because, depravedly, I wish to be her first experience with sex, no matter how rough.

"Why? Are you going to fuck me?"

I look at her mouth again, then farther down to her nipples outlined clearly through the thin fabric of her silvery dress. I stand and move around the desk to kneel in front of her.

I'm so close I can see every blue, green, and gold fleck that gives color to her gray irises. Count every freckle that dusts the bridge of her nose.

Unable to help myself, I lift my hand to her face and brush her long bangs to the side, concentrating on the softness of her skin on my fingertips. She visibly shivers but doesn't pull away. Doesn't blink.

Brave girl.

"I want to fuck you more than I've ever wanted to fuck anyone. Will you let me fuck you, Skye?"

She sucks in a controlled breath and swallows. "Isn't that what I'm here for? So that you can do whatever you want with me?" She might be nervous, but she never looks away, her big, haunting eyes focused intensely on mine. She's beguiling at first glance, seeming naive and innocent, but, really, she's calculating. Like a little lamb aware of its own helplessness as a lion approaches. A lamb willing to do whatever the fuck it takes to stay alive.

"*Is* that why you're here? So that I can do whatever I want with you?" I drop my hand to her lips and trace them.

"If I ask you to open for me and then slide my dick inside your beautiful mouth, would you suck it?"

"Would I have a choice?"

"We all have a choice. You chose to be here. You chose to allow anyone who bought your contract to fuck you, if that's what he or she wanted."

"Then I could choose to say no?" she asks yet doesn't move away when I push my thumb past her lips, past the sharp edge of her teeth to her moist tongue. And, still, her gaze stays locked with mine.

"Suck it," I order, just to see what she'll do. A test.

Her lips wrap around my thumb, encasing it in that warm wetness. She draws it deeper into her mouth, her tongue moving over the tip like it's the head of my dick.

My cock twitches as I imagine that's exactly what she's doing, and I go from rock-hard to steel.

With an inward groan, I tug my thumb from her mouth and stand. She follows me up with that beautiful doe eyed stare that feigns innocence, but with the way she sucked me, there's no denying she's done it before.

"You're not a virgin," I state and move away from her so that I can think clearer.

"No," she says. "I'm not."

I go to the built-in wet bar and grab the scotch decanter tightly, as tightly as I'd like to grasp the neck of the men who've touched her in the past, almost to the breaking point. "Tell me about your indenture. What exactly is it that made you do it?" I pour the amber liquid into a highball glass.

When she remains quiet for a long while, I turn to her. She's staring straight ahead, her breathing still deep and controlled, like the question agitated her, but she's trying not to show it.

She lifts a hand to the delicate collar at her throat and swallows. "You don't know why I'm here?"

"I want to hear it from you."

"I need protection. My father died. His enemies want money from me that I don't have access to yet. They're out there, waiting." She turns her focus to the window.

"What about Maisel?"

Skye's head spins to me. "You know about her?"

"Yes."

There's silence again as she obviously measures her words. "She's been taken care of. It's only me now."

I consider that, wondering what exactly "taken care of" entails but don't push for more. I'll get the truth later. For now, I'm more curious about other things.

"Do you know who I am?" I ask.

For a split second, her attention wanders around the room, then she brings it back to me. "Everyone knows who you are. The Maxtons own half of Philadelphia."

"But do you *know* who I am?" I ask.

She studies me carefully. "You're Arran Maxton."

"Correct." I down the drink in my hand. "I'm also your father's worst enemy."

6

SKYE

"I'm also your father's worst enemy." Arran's words blast through the air like a sonic boom that leaves me deaf to everything else.

I struggle to control my breathing, my chest rising and falling rapidly as I process what he's just said. He's one of my father's enemies? Was I purchased by one of the men I was running from?

"I don't have money." The words spill from me, the fear I've been trying to conceal visible now.

"Thomas didn't owe me money," Arran grinds out.

"W-what did he owe you?"

"My sister's life."

I rear back as if he's slapped me, my fear forgotten. "What are you saying? That my father caused her death?" I shake my head in denial even as my mind rushes through everything I remember hearing about Catherine Maxton's murder two years ago. It was all over the news. How could it not have been? The heiress daughter of the Maxton empire found dead on the stairs of the Vellermo Art Institute. It was the talk of every local news program. Photographs of her naked body were published before the family's lawyers put out a cease and desist.

I was unfortunate enough to see those photographs on my father's desk before he removed them from my sight. And it wasn't Catherine's nudity that had made me gasp in horror. It was the obvious brutality with which she was killed.

"My father would never have—" I begin, but he cuts me off.

"He did."

My teeth clack as I shut my mouth, and it takes all my control to keep it closed. I want to argue with this man. To tell him that though my father was far from perfect, he was no murderer. He could never have done such a thing!

But as much as I loved Daddy, and as much as it pains me to keep quiet, I don't defend his honor. One day I will, but not this day. Today, all I can think about is my little sister. And the thought of her safety brings back that fear I'd forgotten.

"Is that why you bought me?" I ask, my heart in my throat. "To kill me?"

Shit. I don't care about myself, but if he kills me, I won't be able to do what I was sent to do, and Maisie could pay the price for that.

His blue eyes stay on mine and I desperately search for any clue as to his state of mind. I need to know if he's lying when he answers me.

"I don't know why I bought you," he replies, and it rings true, though it's a useless response.

Of course, if he'd said yes, I would fight like an animal. I'd do everything in my power to kill him first. And if he'd said no, I wouldn't believe him. Because if I thought someone was responsible for Maisie's death, I'd tear them apart.

That's when it hits me. What he really wants. Why Gideon was so sure Arran would buy me.

"You want revenge," I whisper.

"Wouldn't you?" he retorts.

I frown, my brows pulled tightly together. "Did you kill my father?"

Smirking, he comes to me once again. This time, he extends his hand to me. I take it and rise to my feet.

Standing so close to me that I'm forced to look up, he tilts his face as if he's considering my question. All the while, he holds on to my hand, his thumb rubbing little circles on my palm.

"I didn't touch Thomas," he finally replies, but I sense there's more to that answer. So much more.

"Regardless," I say. "He's dead. Even if he did something to your sister, revenge would be a moot point."

"Would it? Or could I do something that would have him rolling in his grave?"

"What could you do?"

Arran leans in further, his mouth just inches from mine. His gaze drops to my lips and the sudden hunger in his expression has me sucking in a breath. "I can think of a few things I could do to you."

His nearness affects me. I'm not stupid enough to deny the fact that I'm insanely attracted to him. I can't control my response to him any more than I could control the effect of fire on my skin. In fact, the reaction is quite similar.

I'm sweating. Practically melting. Every part of my body that's making contact with him burns. Flames lick the inside of my belly as his clean male scent invades my nostrils, and my blood rushes white-hot to every part of me made for sex.

"Dumb is trying to hide evidence. Smart is using it to your advantage." I heard Daddy say to a colleague after they won the case for a woman who killed her husband in self-defense. The other man wanted to hide the fact that she'd been abused. Daddy knew it was the only thing that would set her free.

What he said stuck with me. I held on to it, thinking I'd use it someday to defend someone like that woman. I'm using it to protect myself instead.

I allow Arran to see what he does to me. Let him see the quickening of my breaths, the rise and fall of my breasts as they graze his chest. I do nothing to shield the flush in my cheeks or even the slight tremble caused by the fear that he'll hurt me.

In fact, I embrace all those things because I'm a smart girl and I know what it's going to take to get a man like him to give me what I need.

"You're going to fuck me," I say, inflecting submission into my tone.

Lifting his free hand, he touches the skin of my arm, trailing his fingertips over my shoulder and collar, then around to the back of my neck. I shiver at the contact, and he smiles, seemingly pleased.

He brings his lips to my ear and whispers, "I'm going to do more than fuck you, Skye. I'm going to make you beg me to fuck you. I'm going to make you come on my fingers and in my mouth, and when I fuck you, it will be because you ask me to. Then it will be *you* who betrays your father. *You* who curses him to hell for what he's done. And the best part is, you'll do it willingly because you'd rather save your-self than remain true to him. Won't you?"

"Yes." My hands fist just out of sight, and I bite back what I really want to say. That I will let him do whatever he wants, but not for me. For Maisie.

"But do me a favor. Drop the bullshit timid act. I don't buy it."

I stiffen at his words. "What?"

Pulling away from me only far enough to peer intensely into my eyes, he grins. A terrifyingly beautiful grin that is so sure of what he's just said. "Ah, there's that defiance."

"It's not in my nature to be submissive," I admit, hoping that one truth will be enough to have him stop searching for more.

"And that, Skye, is what will make it so much more fun. Because when you ask me to fuck you, you're going to mean it. I'll know if you don't." He smiles again, but it vanishes as he takes in my features and says, "You are so beautiful." His tone is soft and alluring, but something darkens in the depths of his blue eyes, and I wonder if it angers him that he finds me pretty.

"Are you going to hurt me?" is the only thing I have left to ask.

"Only if you want me to." He runs the back of his hand over my cheek. "Let's get you showered."

Grabbing my wrist, he spins on his heel and tugs me through the house to a bedroom on the second floor. Judging by the grandeur of the suite, which has a king-size mahogany sleigh bed fit for royalty and large, bulky furni-ture, I'd say it's his room. It reeks of wealth and power and overbearing masculinity.

It's on the tip of my tongue to tell him the space could benefit from a bouquet of flowers or a damned frilly pillow when he takes me into the bathroom and I'm left speechless.

The complete opposite of the darkness of his bedroom, the bath is light and airy. A long white marble counter floats on one wall. There is no tub; however, it does have one of the largest glass-enclosed showers I've seen in my life, with not one, but two showerheads and a waterfall spout on the ceiling.

Fluffy towels are rolled up and stacked on a teak bench, and on a table located inside the shower are perhaps the only flowers in the entire home.

"You have orchids." It comes out as more of a confused statement than a question.

"I don't have time to care for them properly, and someone suggested I put them in here so they get misted daily." He opens the glass door and turns on the jets.

When he returns to me, I'm still staring at the many pots of flowers. They look good. Healthy. There's a pair of pruning shears and a dead bud on the counter, as if he's just recently clipped them. Suddenly, I'm somewhere else, staring at pink shears and flowery gardening gloves.

"I hear taking care of orchids is a calming hobby," I say tightly, my throat constricting on the memory of my mother's garden.

"Kate was the one with the hobby. I inherited it."

My brow furrows. And just as I'm wondering why anyone would inherit a hobby—because why not just let the flowers die—he reaches for the hem of my dress, and I jolt, slapping his hands away on instinct. When he narrows his eyes, I realize my mistake.

"I'm sorry. Usually, I undress myself."

Without taking his gaze off mine, he takes the hem again and lifts it clear over my head in one fell swoop.

My hair falls back over my shoulders but doesn't do me the favor of also covering my breasts. Not that it could. It's not long enough and my D-cups would require a lot more of it to be concealed.

Then he hooks my thong and easily pulls it past my hips, letting it pool at my feet.

An instant hot flash spreads over my skin as Arran takes a step back and drops his stare to my body. He takes it all in, his gaze trailing over every inch of me as I stand here naked, like a fucking offering. A piece of meat he wants to devour.

Something he's just bought and is ready to consume.

Then he's the one undressing, and I'm not sure what's worse. Being exposed to him or him baring his masculine perfection to me. His tall, lean swimmer's body. The breadth of his chest and shoulders, muscled and fit, but not overly bulky. The light matting of golden hair that covers his chest and thickens the lower it goes, over his tight abdomen and even thicker still to...

I flick my eyes upward and catch his grin. "I told you I'm not a virgin. I've seen what you have before."

"Have you?"

Not exactly, I want to say. The men I've been with have been more manageable looking.

He takes me by the wrist and tugs me into the shower. Swirling steam rises as the water heats, engulfing us and the orchids on the table. I glance at the pretty flowers as Arran moves me under the jets, and they seem only too happy to be in here with him day after day. They belong to him too, and even though he doesn't care *for* them, he does take care *of* them. He keeps them safe.

Oddly enough, the thought makes me relax a little. That and the water streaming down my body, warming away any lingering trembles.

I have to believe that if he were going to kill me, he would have done it already.

But that's not all that has you shaking, is it?

He grabs a bottle with a French label on it. The scent of lavender and tea tree rises with the steam as he squirts a dab of the product onto his hand. Then he rubs his palms together and digs his fingers into my hair.

I shut my eyes and drop my head back as he massages my scalp and works his fingertips from my temples to the base of my neck.

It takes a lot of effort not to moan. To keep from begging him not to stop.

With his thumbs, he deftly works the tension from my shoulders and down my spine. Then his fingers trail feather light over my ribs as he pulls me against him.

In my haze, it takes me a moment to realize how intimately we're pressed together. How he's practically engulfed me with his size and that my entire backside is to his front.

My eyes fly open when I feel him harden, the length of his shaft pressed to my ass crack. He's big and hot and the very idea of that inside me sends a needful pulse straight to my core.

Soapy hands cup my breasts and immediately begin to toy with my nipples. This time, I do moan. I can't help it. The wetness and the soap is increasing every sensation tenfold.

As he teases and pinches my nipples, he begins a rhythmic thrusting of his dick between my legs. It slides across my entrance but doesn't penetrate. What it does do is keep me on edge, wondering when exactly he's going to ram it home.

He doesn't. Instead, he turns me so that I'm facing him.

Kneeling, he wraps his arms around my back and tugs me until my breasts are in his face.

Before I can react, he latches onto a nipple, sending a wave of heat to my belly. When he moves to the other, my knees nearly buckle. It's the way he's sucking and licking and biting that has me weak and moaning out of control.

But it's when his fingers find their way to my wet and swollen clit that I truly feel like I might fall. With a gasp, I bend over his blond head and place my hands on his shoulders.

I'm going to come like this, with Arran's mouth on my breasts and fingers barely even grazing my pussy. My belly is molten and quivering and all I need is one more...

Suddenly, he stops. I'm panting, practically wheezing, and he just stops.

"Ask me to make you come." His deep, guttural request sounds more like an animalistic growl than a human voice. He looks up at me. "Say my name."

Confused, unable to process anything more than the denial of physical release, I peer into his blue eyes.

He touches the tip of my clit, just barely, but enough to make me suck in a breath. Up and down, he rubs the nub that's so swollen, it's sticking out beyond the labia.

I stiffen, on the verge of that orgasm again, and he stops yet again.

"Tell me, Skye. If you want to come, ask for it."

"And if I don't?"

Arran leans in and takes a nipple into his mouth and groans, sending vibrations though me like an electric jolt. "I'm hoping you won't. I quite enjoy torturing you like this. It makes my fucking dick harder than it's ever been."

I want to deny him the satisfaction of hearing me beg

him to make me come. And for a few minutes of that sweet and cruel torture, I endure.

But I was too close already, so when it starts again, not even he can stop me from climaxing.

"Oh God!" I cry out.

He tries to pull his hand away, but I grab hold of it and keep it pressed between my legs as I grind my pussy onto it. The orgasm is so explosive, I'm nearly blinded. I drop my face onto the top of Arran's head, heaving and moaning until the waves of pleasure begin to ebb.

I keep his wrist tightly clutched between my fingers and his hand on my sex, squeezing him with each lingering pulse.

When it's over, my whole body is trembling. I don't move away from him, because I need to stave the tears threatening to form in my eyes as shame fills me.

I didn't have to ask him to make me come. Didn't have to say his name. It wasn't necessary. I was one hundred percent aware that it was Arran's hand, and I took it anyway, then I rubbed myself with it until I came.

Shit. I came on my father's enemy. He made me come. His face, his body, his touch.

"This was cruel," I whisper into his hair.

"Life is cruel." He stands and looks at me without a bit of regret. "Stay here for a few minutes. Enjoy the shower. I'll get the room ready."

Stepping out, he leaves me to dwell on what I've just done. But I don't remain for long. After turning off the jets, I grab one of the fluffy rolled-up towels and wrap it around myself.

When I go into the master suite, I find Arran pulling back the blankets on the bed. "We've both had a long day. Let's get some rest."

"I don't have anything to wear," I say.

"While you're in my bed, you won't need anything."

He pulls the sheets back and motions for me to slip under them. Then he leans in and tightens the blankets around me. "In case you get any ideas, I'm a very light sleeper."

"What ideas would I get?" I don't move. Can't even breathe as I wonder what he's about. Will he tease me again the way he did in the shower? Will he fuck me now?

To my surprise, he does something worse. Which is nothing. Simply goes to the other side of the bed, gets in, and turns out the light. "Dream of me, Skye."

Within minutes, he's out, his breathing even and deep. Yet I remain awake for hours, my nerves frazzled and my body humming with expectation. I'm afraid to fall asleep in the enemy's bed, a part of me expecting to wake up with his hands around my throat and another part hoping he'll want to finish what he started in the shower.

I bury my head in the overstuffed pillow, not wanting to think of the shame that brings me. That I enjoyed his large hands on my body, that he was able to make me come so quickly when the few men I've slept with have mostly failed. The two guys I did orgasm with can't even get the credit, because it took a lot of concentration and dirty thoughts on my part to get there.

But Arran...

He made me come. And even though I hadn't spoken the words, inside, I begged for it. I wanted him to get me there.

To my horror, I discovered he was right. The moment it was over, I knew I'd betrayed my father. Because not once did I push Arran away. I clung to him, held his hand to me, rocked shamelessly against it.

I sigh. My attraction to this villain isn't important. What is important is that he's attracted to me. There's no doubt about that. He wants me, and that's going to be my ticket to getting the information Gideon wants.

And then Maisie will be freed.

7

MAISIE

I follow the sound of hushed voices echoing through the halls of my dark prison. Well, it doesn't look much like a prison and it's not dark. Actually, it's more like a fancy hotel. The kind with a luxury spa, where everything is white and cream and you wear robes and cucumbers under your eyes.

It's a far cry from the place Gideon first took Skye and me to, which was so over the top dungeon-like, with cinder block walls and iron doors, I'm beginning to think he read a book called *Villain 101* and copied what he saw just to scare us into complying. But even he must have been grossed out by the dinginess, because two minutes after Skye left, I was brought here.

Stopping a few feet before I get to the kitchen, I slip out of my sneakers and tiptoe closer.

"How much did she go for?" the blonde girl I've heard referred to as Scar asks.

"A mil," Gideon replies.

She whistles. "I called it. I knew it would be more than a hundred K. You owe me ten."

"I'll add it to your next paycheck."

"Correction. *I* will add it to my next paycheck. You'll conveniently forget."

"Will I?" he chuckles.

"The question is, will he kill her? If he does, you owe me ten more."

My stomach tightens and a ball the size of an orange forms in my throat, making it hard to breathe. Kill her? Kill Skye? Is that what they're saying? Why would Arran Maxton want to kill Skye? The whole reason I didn't put up more of a fight was because he said she'd be safe!

"He won't kill her," he says, and my heart slows a little. "He'll want to, but his sense of morality won't let him go that far."

Scar laughs. "What fucking sense of morality? Didn't you see what he did to Yegor?"

"Yegor deserved far worse. Imogen does not." There's the sound of a chair being pushed, followed by footsteps, and I quickly move around the corner. "I have to go."

"What do you mean you have to go?"

"I mean I have to go," he says.

"All right. I'll go get the kid."

"Maisel is staying here."

She laughs again, but this time, it sounds fake. "I'm sorry. I must have wax in my ears, because I thought I heard you say she's staying. But, of course, you're taking her with you, right?"

"No can do. I have too much shit to get done to babysit."

"What you really mean is, you don't want a kid around while you play with your little captive bird."

My ears perk up. Another captive? And here I thought we were special.

"You didn't have a problem with me playing with my captive bird before," Gideon retorts.

"That's because you weren't trying to pawn off a kid on me. Take her with you. I'm sure she'll get along with Sofia just fine." She's not laughing now. In fact, she sounds angry.

"Maisel will be more comfortable here. And what I'm doing with Sofia is so much more than playing." His voice goes real low, the way Daddy's used to get when he was giving us a last-chance warning.

"Ugh. I'm starting to think it's the other way around. Men get stupid with certain women. You think she's at your mercy, but I've seen the look in her eyes, Gid. She's a cornered animal just waiting for the chance to bite." I hear the clacking of teeth and imagine she's just mimicked the motion.

Now it's he who laughs. "I fucking hope she bites me. It'll give me a reason to bite back."

More footsteps, then they stop near the foyer. I dare a peek and spot the two of them facing each other by the door. Him towering over her. Her glaring up at him.

"I don't know anything about kids," Scar continues to argue.

"What's there to know? All you have to do is make sure she has food and water," Gideon says.

"I'm not a pet," I blurt out, stepping fully into view. "You don't just leave me bowls of food and water."

Scar points at me. "Do you see that? I told her to stay put. She doesn't listen. Do you want me to lock her up?"

I roll my eyes. "It's not like I left the condo. Chill. If he wants to go take care of his other prisoners, let him. I'll behave."

Gideon's lips pull up and I can't help my heart flipping

in my chest or the little sigh that escapes me. For an old dude, he's insanely hot, with jet-black hair and ice-blue eyes.

"You wouldn't happen to have a seventeen-year-old brother, would you, Giddy?" I ask, liking the tic he gets in his jaw.

His smile vanishes and Scar bursts out laughing.

"Maybe this *will* be fun after all," she says.

He glowers at her, then turns it on me. "I've asked you three times to stop calling me that. I'm Mr. Black to you. Learn some respect, Maisel."

"Yeah. Skye always tells me to respect my elders. But seeing as you kidnapped us..." I raise my brows and dip my head in a you-fill-in-the-blank sort of way.

Laughing again, Scarlet says, "She doesn't listen."

Gideon turns back to her and pats her on the shoulder, saying, "Good luck," before he leaves.

For a long while, she stands there, staring after him. As if he abandoned her when she needed him the most. It makes me feel a little sorry for her.

"Am I that scary? I mean, I can wipe myself. Feed myself. Put myself to bed. Really, for a prisoner, I'm easy." I shrug.

Her shoulders slump. "Something tells me that's not exactly true."

"I'll prove it." I make my way to the kitchen with her in tow. "What do you have to eat around here?"

"Wine," she replies, leaning against the counter. "Cheese, maybe."

I open the fridge. The very empty fridge, save for half a bottle of wine. "Yikes."

"I'm a busy woman. I eat out a lot," she says defensively.

My stomach growls, which is weird because a second ago, I was perfectly fine. Guess realizing there's no food has suddenly made me hungry. "Can we order in? Or do you like to keep this place super secret? I won't scream for help when the delivery comes. I swear." I raise three scout's honor fingers.

She rolls her eyes at me. "Kid, if you screamed when the delivery came, I'd throw you out there and then you'd really be screwed."

"Wouldn't Giddy be mad at you, then? I'm his trump card." I grin widely.

"He'd get over it." She tugs her phone from her pocket. "What do you like?"

"John's Chinese."

"John's Chinese?" She laughs. "Are you serious?"

"It's authentic. I promise. And most importantly, fast."

She searches it. "Huh. Has great reviews."

"Get me the lo mein and pork fried rice."

"Please," she says.

Frowning, I ask, "Please what?"

"Ugh. Never mind." She dials the number and orders our food.

Half an hour later, there's a knock at the door. Scar pulls out her phone again and opens up a screen that shows the camera feed from just outside. But even after having seen who's there, she approaches carefully, her hand twitching over the knife holstered to her thigh and ready to pull it.

When she opens the door, she says something in a low tone to the guy and accepts the food from him.

"That's not one of the usual delivery guys," I say.

"No. That's one of my guys. I'd never allow anyone else up here."

"Scar, are you an assassin?" I ask, following her back into the kitchen. "You look like an assassin."

She places our delivery on the counter and slides my box to me, along with chopsticks and packets of sauce. "What does an assassin look like? And it's Miss Scarlet to you."

"Scarlet. I like it. You look more like a Scarlet than a Scar." I open my to-go container and immediately begin shoving noodles into my mouth as I observe her taking dainty bites of her stir fry.

She moves her food closer and sits at the bar beside me. "So what makes you think I'm an assassin?"

"Well"—I slurp a noodle—"besides the obvious?"

She frowns. "What's obvious?"

"You hang out with men who kill people, and you're dressed super sleek. Black leather pants, black turtleneck, your hair is smoothed back," I tick off on my fingers one by one. "And you have a huge knife strapped to your thigh."

"Oh." Scarlet glances down as if she'd forgotten it was there. "That's what you're basing it on? My clothes and a blade I use as protection?"

"I'll prove it. Can I have my bag back? I'm sure you've already snooped all through it anyway."

She gives me a curious stare and laughs. "Sure."

After disappearing for a few minutes, she returns with it and hands it to me. "I kept your cell phone. You can have it back when this is all over."

Huffing, I say, "Whatever."

I dig through my bag until I find my sketchpad, then flip through the pages in search of a specific one.

"You draw cartoons?" she asks.

I pause and give her my most evil glare. "Comics," I reply, hitting the *c*'s especially hard.

Her lips quirk. "Comics."

"This one." I point. "See? You kind of look like her. The black clothes, blonde hair. She even has green eyes like you."

Scarlet's brows pinch together as she peers at the woman I drew a few years ago. She sits beside me again as she reaches for the pad and pulls it closer. "*Rage,*" she reads the name on the top of the page. "You drew this?"

"Yes."

"Wow, Maisel—"

"Maisie. I prefer to be called Maisie. I was named after my two grandmothers. Maisel Eudora. It's like their dream for me was to be an old lady." I cringe. Thank God Skye gave me a cute nickname.

Scarlet turns to me. "You're really good, Maisie." But even though she gives me the compliment, she seems disturbed, and I wonder if I made a mistake in showing her.

"Thanks."

"Tell me about her. Why did you name her Rage?"

I try to remember all the details as I saw them in my head when I created Rage a few years ago. "Her parents were murdered in front of her. Her brother was able to take them out of the house and cared for her for a few years. Then he was found and killed by the same people. She was sent to a home, where she was abused. She ran away and turned to a life of crime and became one of the deadliest assassins. That was until she was assigned to take out a family that had a son and a daughter, and it reminded her of her own family. She saved them instead and became an antihero."

"Antihero?"

"Yeah, you know, a bad guy who does good things."

She laughs, pauses to glance at the drawing, then

laughs harder, literally bending over the bar. "Kid, you really *are* young. There's no such thing as a bad person who does good deeds. Everything we do is bad." Shoving the book back to me, she continues to eat.

I stare at her for a long while, my appetite completely gone, even for John's Chinese. Part of me is pissed off that she laughed at me. I've always hated being made fun of. The other part of me is scared that she might be right. That bad people aren't capable of kindness. Because if that's true...

"Scarlet?"

"Hmm."

"Is my sister going to be okay?"

She turns to me, and in her eyes, I see pity. "She'll be fine," she says, proving to me the one thing bad people are best at. Lying.

8

SKYE

The day my mother died, I was afraid to fall asleep. I was so scared I'd be haunted by terrible dreams. But that night, both Maisie and I snuggled into Daddy's arms and we all slept soundly. Deeply.

Exhaustion does do that to me. I think it's a protective mechanism my brain uses to remain functional when conscious. It sends me into a deathlike rest. Though I'm not sure what's worse. Dreams or being completely unaware of my existence.

I wake slowly, coming out of that kind of deep sleep I go into after a traumatic event.

It takes me a moment to orient myself, peeling my eyes open, searching the darkness for the usual markers I find in my room—the blue light from the digital clock on my nightstand, a window to my right, and the lazy circling of the fan above me.

All of those things are absent. It's not that I expected them to be there. I have no delusions that everything that's happened was a dream. Although it *is* a nightmare.

What is there is Arran's hard body pressed to my back and his strong arm snaked around my waist. His hand is tucked under my right breast, fitting there perfectly, and his warm breath is on the back of my neck.

I'm not sure how long we've been locked together like this. When I finally drifted off, we were at opposite sides of the king-size bed. Did Arran knowingly bring me closer to him? Or is this just a product of two people seeking heat?

Whatever it was, it wasn't enough to rouse me. I was too tired and emotionally drained. Actually, I don't think a bomb going off near my ear would've done the job.

Well, I'm awake now and very much aware of the man at my back. Of his scent enveloping me.

Then he shifts slightly, and his cock presses between my ass cheeks. Though I can tell he's not fully erect, it still brings back images of the things he did to me in the shower. The way he insinuated his dick so close to my entrance and made me crave something I shouldn't.

Fuck me, I wanted it. I wonder if I'd never been with a man before, known what it feels like to be filled and stretched, if I still would have wanted it. I want to lie to myself, but it would do me no good.

Arran moves against me once more. Suddenly, I'm not just sleep warmed, but hot. My belly tightens and I feel the need to squirm against him.

Fuck this!

Carefully, I attempt to pull away, but his arm tightens around me and he digs one of his legs between mine.

I try again, and this time, not only do I fail, but I also get his hand cupped over my breast. My nipple puckers against his palm and I groan inwardly.

Is he awake and playing a game with me?

No. As far as I can tell, he's completely out. His breathing is steady and deep, and though he's managed to keep me securely nestled against his chest, his hold slackens if I don't move.

I roll my eyes. So much for being a light sleeper. Stupid threat. I could probably take off my collar and strangle him with it and he wouldn't stir.

Now there's an appealing thought. But far too risky.

For two hours, I remain in that hell, staring toward the window, waiting for the light of day to slip between the thick curtains.

It's easy to tell the moment he does finally wake. His dick goes from slightly hard to steel and he inhales, taking in the scent of the skin of my neck.

I shut my eyes in hopes that he'll leave me alone, and for a moment, he does. But the moment doesn't last.

He begins to trail small wet kisses from my ear to my shoulder, then bites me there at the same time that he moves his cock so that it slides over my ass crack and between my legs.

I can't help the soft sigh that escapes me. It's impossible to prevent it when he does that to my over-sensitized skin.

"You're awake," he says, his voice made hoarser with sleep.

"Yes," I can barely reply as he starts to graze my nipples with his fingertips. Back and forth he goes between the two, circling them, making me pant.

"Ask me to fuck you, Skye."

"Fuck me," I whisper.

Laughing, he shakes his head. "Say it like you mean it."

"I can't."

"Not yet. But you will." He slides the blankets off my body and lifts himself so that he's looking down at me.

Although it's not very bright in the room, enough sunlight is spilling through the part between the curtain panels that I'm sure he can see me clearly. In fact, he confirms it when he begins to draw lines between the freckles on my hip.

"Roll onto your back," he says.

I do as he says but keep my arm across my breasts and my legs closed.

A smile creeps over his lips as he grabs my wrist and moves it away. Heat spreads through my chest as he touches every inch of it with his eyes, hungrily taking it all in.

With his big hands, he cups my tits, enveloping them in heat. He pushes them together and bends down to take first one nipple into his mouth, then the other, and then both. I gasp and moan, writhing beneath him.

"You're very sensitive here, aren't you?" he asks.

I bite my lower lip, wanting to deny it but unable to utter a word when he sucks on them again.

They *are* sensitive. Always have been. But even so, I've never had anyone work to drive me to the brink of insanity like this. He licks and bites, giving as much attention to the soft skin under my breast as the nipples themselves.

Just when I think I might go crazy or, worse, come from this alone, he stops. "Not yet. I want to know what you taste like when you come."

Sitting up, he slides his hands down my ribcage and waist, then between my knees to part them. I feel my pussy part too, exposing my clit and entrance fully to him, and the way his jaw tightens, like he has to use a great deal of restraint not to pounce, has me aching.

His gaze follows his movement as he touches me softly, almost reverently, from my clit to my entrance. "You have the most beautiful cunt, Skye. Did you know that?" He lifts those intense blues to me. "So fucking beautiful."

I suck in air when he leans in and his breath fans across my sex, moist, hot, and intense. Pushing myself up on my elbows, my eyes glued to his mouth, I watch with an almost tangible anticipation as he brings it to my pussy.

When he does, he shuts his lids and moans as if he's never tasted anything sweeter. The sight of it, his broad shoulders against the backs of my legs, his head between them, of him sucking me, his nose buried in my pubic hair is almost too much.

Dropping back onto the bed, I dig my fingers into his thick blond hair and hold him there. An almost violent need to come overwhelms me, and I begin to thrust my hips upward aggressively. But I'm not worried about the possibility of asphyxiating him. Not when he chuckles in that low tone that rumbles through me. It annoys the shit out of me, and the desire to kick him clears away some of the lust haze that makes it so damned hard to think when he touches me.

In that moment of clarity, I recall the sobering reality that hit me the last time he made me come. The guilt of allowing it to someone who calls my father enemy, who wished revenge on him and me.

I want to scream at him to stop. To leave me the hell alone so that I can live with myself today. He'd do it.

But my throat is too tight and, instead, what comes out is his name on a moan.

As if he can detect the shift in me, he doubles his efforts, his fingers slipping deep inside, searching for that spot. When he finds it, I jolt, and within seconds, I'm being flung over the edge. I come in relentless waves that have me screaming and clawing at the sheets and gasping for air all at the same time.

Arran gets to his knees and moves closer, his thighs pushing against the backs of my legs. "Ask me to fuck you, Skye," he says as he presses the head of his cock over my entrance.

I cry out from the contact on my still-pulsing flesh.

"Ask me to fuck you," he repeats, his dick sliding up and down over my clit.

I'm in that mindless fog, unable to speak and glad for it because if I could, I'd say yes. Yes, fuck me. Fill me. Make me come again.

But I'm saved the horror of begging the enemy to fuck me when he tightens his fist around his cock and begins to pump. Faster and faster he does it, until cum shoots from the head and covers my belly.

When he's done, he looks at the mess he's made. "That cum should be inside you, Skye. It should be spilling from your pretty pussy. When you ask me to fuck you, I'll never come anywhere else."

The shame of reaching my climax, of giving Arran exactly what he wants, is too fresh, and my words come out with a bite. "I'll never ask you to fuck me and mean it. So just do it if that's what you're after. You know I won't fight you."

"Because *you* need protection."

I hesitate to reply, not liking something in his statement. "Yes."

A crease forms between his brows as his gaze searches mine. Then, without another word, he gets up and disappears into the bathroom. Several minutes later, he returns with a moist towel. He's about to clean me up but seems to think better of it.

Then he swipes a fingertip across the wetness, gathering some of it, and brings it to my lips. "Lick it."

Almost of its own accord, my tongue darts out. The taste of his male essence is like a drug, warming me instantly. A flush spreads over my cheeks and through my body as I clean his finger.

Arran's gaze glasses over, like he's hypnotized as he watches me lick him. He pulls out and gathers more of his cum off my belly and brings it to my lips. "Again."

I clean him off once more, this time shutting my eyes the same way he did when he ate me. Now I understand why he did it. Because as much as he might hate me, his body doesn't. Just like me, he craves what he shouldn't.

We taste good to each other.

"When I come back later, you're doing this to my dick," he says gruffly.

He pulls his finger out again, and I watch as he goes to the bathroom, leaving the door open. I remain in bed, staring in that direction, wondering if it's an invitation to go in. An order. Neither.

I'm about to stand but stop when the doorbell rings. Arran comes out with a towel wrapped around his waist and rivulets of water dripping from his hair and rolling down his naked chest.

I make a little sound in my throat and avert my gaze. This physical attraction is a damned curse. "You have a guest."

"Charles will get it." From the closet, he takes out a gray suit and dresses in it.

"Where are you going?" I ask, holding the sheets to my chest.

"I have several meetings this morning." He goes to the wood armoire with mirrored panels and pulls out a silvery-blue tie, then closes the door and peers into his reflection as he puts it on.

"Will you be gone long?"

"Several hours. Make yourself at home. The fridge and pantry are stocked if you get hungry."

"I can explore the house?"

He peers at me through the mirror and makes a final adjustment to his tie. Then he turns to me. "You can go anywhere you'd like. Open any drawers. I keep nothing here that needs to be guarded. Well, except for you."

I roll my eyes. "You know what I mean. Can I roam freely, or do you have any rooms I need to avoid?"

"Go wherever you'd like," he repeats. "I should warn you, there are cameras in the entire home, except for the bedrooms. But none of the doors are locked. You may leave the house. Charles will not stop you. Though I wouldn't if I were you."

Nodding, I get out of bed and get my dress from the bathroom. As I tug it over my head, he stops me. "What, you want me naked all day?"

"As much as the idea of coming home to you in nothing but this collar pleases me"—he touches the diamond chain around my neck—"I'd hate for any of my men to see you through the windows."

"Why? Are you the jealous type?" It's a question meant to tease, but the sudden intensity in his gaze has me swallowing hard.

He comes to me, pressing himself against my body. To my horror, I sink into him as he brings his lips to my ear. "I am, Skye. I don't share what's mine in any way. And you are that. Even if I haven't fucked you yet, you're mine."

I want to bristle over the possessive tone in his voice, but I don't. Instead, the part of me that doesn't care about female empowerment seems to delight in his words. And it's that part of me that's in control when I place the palm of my hand on his chest and gaze up at him through my lashes. "What would you do if someone saw me naked?"

Without hesitation, he replies, "I'd carve their eyes out."

9

SKYE

fter Arran leaves, and with his permission, I dig through his closet in search of anything that will fit. I slip into a T-shirt and pair of sweatpants. At five foot seven, I'm considered tall for a woman. But even with my height, I have to roll up the bottoms.

While I'm in the closet, I take advantage. He said there are no cameras in here, and I hope it wasn't a lie, because I really dig. I open drawers and snoop through pockets and on the shelves. I'm not sure what I hope to find, mainly because I've never spied on anyone. I'll take anything that can give me a clue as to where Arran could be keeping his father.

Half an hour later, I'm standing empty-handed in the middle of his suite. Nothing. Not a fucking clue.

Arran said there's nothing hidden but warned me there are cameras throughout the house. Could he have said that just to keep me from looking in the first place? I mean, who doesn't keep personal and private things in their homes? Secret things?

For a moment, I wonder if perhaps Clive is being kept

here. But just as quickly as the thought enters my mind, I dismiss it. There's no way Arran would have me freely strolling around his house if I could discover his father.

Either way, I have no choice but to give myself a tour of his lavish home.

First, I explore all six of the bedrooms and the sitting area on the second floor. Although I don't find anything of interest, it's easy to tell he doesn't have company often. Everything seems untouched and unlived-in. No indentions in the perfectly fluffed pillows or anyone's lingering scent.

The first floor isn't much different—with a dining room I doubt has been used in months and a formal living room with sofas that seem as inviting as sitting on a cactus.

I go into the kitchen, not because I'm hungry, but because I need to appear to be doing something other than searching. There is food in the pantry, though not much. I sit for a while at the long island counter, taking my time with an almond butter sandwich.

When I'm done, I continue my "tour." I enter Arran's study, which is where I've been dying to go from the start. If there's anything at all, it will be here.

I don't see the cameras, which doesn't mean they can't see *me*. So I piddle around, slowly making my way around the perimeter, eyeing everything on the bookshelves. Just in case there are any hidden panels, I touch everything, running my palms over books, knickknacks, and the decorative carvings on the moldings.

My heart pounds in my chest when I sit behind his desk, my fingers twitching as I stare at the handles on the drawers. Do I dare open them? Shit, where the hell are the cameras in this place?

Sweat begins to form on my upper lip and nose from the

stress. I'm not cut out to be a spy. I'm a fucking law student in distress!

I hook my finger through one of the handles and pull and nearly vomit from the anxiety. When I peer into the drawer and find it empty, I want to scream.

Why did Gideon send me here? What made him think I was the right person for this? Yes, I'm smart. Book smart. This job requires a completely different sort of smarts.

He didn't send you because of your brains.

I pull open another drawer. It has plain white paper and a stapler.

Gideon didn't send me here for my brain, I know that now. He sent me here because of my name. Because I'm a Cameron. Did he assume Arran would want my body? Or was that just a bonus?

Opening another drawer, I consider that question. It would have been impossible for Gideon to know with certainty that Arran would be attracted to me. He wouldn't have bet on that.

I lift my gaze from the desk and look to the spot on the floor where I sat for hours yesterday. Arran watched me from here, wondering what the hell to do with me. Throw me out to meet my doom, keep me. Kill me himself.

Something tells me he hasn't quite decided on that last one yet.

As if the photograph of his family calls to me, I turn my attention to it. I stand and walk to the bookshelf where it sits. Yesterday, I could barely make out the figures. Now is my chance to really look.

If I had known I was going to end up here, maybe I would have studied up more on the Maxton family. But as I didn't have any notion that my future included an indenture to Arran, I have only the random rumors and news stories I've heard and can remember.

There is Clive with his arm around a much younger woman. One of his ex-wives whose name would have eluded me even if he didn't have like ten of them. From what I understand, one of his favorite pastimes was marrying beautiful women several years younger than himself.

A foot away from him is Landon, the eldest of the Maxton children. He resembles Arran, physically, at least. Same height, blond hair, blue eyes. But there's an edge to Arran that's missing in Landon. His gaze isn't as intense, his jawline is much softer, and he doesn't have that perpetual scowl that's on Arran's face even when he's laughing.

That's because he's never laughing in amusement, I remind myself. Only out of sarcasm.

On the other side of Clive is Arran, his arm protectively around Catherine's shoulders. I stare into her delicate face. She also looks like Arran, same coloring. But there's a sweetness to her that shines through.

I wonder how old she was when this picture was taken. When she died, I recall the news saying she was twenty-five. Then I wonder how old Arran is. Thirty? Thirty-two?

They must have been close, not in age necessarily, but as siblings. Although I must admit it's hard to imagine a man like him ever being close to someone. But their body language says otherwise. She was his little sister.

I think of Maisie and what I would do to prevent anyone from hurting her. What I'd do if they did. The truth is, I wouldn't have the restraint Arran has. I'd go batshit crazy and kill whoever was responsible. Even though I'm not a violent person and really have no idea how I'd go about it, I wouldn't rest until I saw them dead and buried.

But would I go after that person's family?

"Hello."

"Jesus!" Startled, I jump away from the bookshelf at the same time as I whirl to the sound of the male voice behind me. For a split second, I mistake him for Arran. However, I quickly realize that the man standing at the doorway isn't Arran, but his brother.

"I'm sorry, I didn't mean to frighten you," he says. His blue eyes, so much like Arran's in color, might lack the intensity of his stare but make up for it in interest. He takes me in, from head to bare toes, pausing at my breasts, and smiles. "I'm Landon. And you must be Imogen?"

Aware that my braless chest is outlined too well by the white T-shirt, I snatch my arms over my breasts uncomfortably. His smile broadens and confirms that, indeed, he saw more than I wanted him to.

"Arran didn't tell me anyone would be stopping by," I say.

Landon moves into the study, his gait casual as he comes closer. "That's probably because I didn't tell him I was coming. Thought I'd just pop in and say hi. Meet you in person."

"Meet *me*?" My heart rate increases. Something in his tone and the keen twinkle in his gaze has me raising my guard instantly. Though he doesn't seem like a threat, I'm not taking any chances. Nonchalantly, I step behind the desk, pretending to straighten the few items on it.

His eyes follow. "I heard you were at Asta last night."

"There were a lot of us at Asta."

"But only one daughter of a certain Judge Thomas Cameron, may he rest in peace." He narrows his gaze, then he scratches his chin as he ponders me. "I was asking myself why Arran bought you. Especially given our... *dicey* history with Thomas."

Shit. Shit. Shit! He knows who I am. And if Arran blames my father for Catherine's death, I'm sure Landon does too.

"Arran should be back any minute," I say, extremely uneasy now. "You can ask him why he bought my contract."

"I don't have to ask. I can see why he did." There's no mistaking his salacious stare for anything else. "Tell me about the contract. How long will you be here?"

"A while," I reply, watching as he goes to a cabinet.

He opens it to display several rows of liquor bottles. "Let's see what new drinks he's acquired. Ah, this one." Taking a whiskey, he pours some into a highball glass and sips. "There's no denying my little brother has good taste. I sample his things from time to time, see if there's anything I want for myself."

"Does he know that? Arran told me he doesn't like to share." I step out of from behind the safety of the desk and move closer to the door.

Landon turns to me and seems amused by my question. "Well, I won't tell him if you won't." He takes a step toward me, and I take one back.

Giving him as pleasant a smile as I can muster, I say, "Why don't you wait here for him. I'm sure he won't be long. I have to go get changed."

I don't get to the door before his hand clamps around my arm and pulls me back. He pushes me against the wall, one of his long legs between mine. I try to shove him away, but he's like a brick wall in front of me.

"Fuck, you're pretty," he whispers hoarsely. Then he leans in and presses his nose to my hair. "You smell fucking good. So fucking good."

"Let me go, Landon. I don't like this," I say, glaring at

him. "And neither will Arran."

He laughs. "Arran has never given a fuck about girls. He's definitely not going to care about a whore."

My palm slams against his cheek. "I'm not a whore."

His fingers are around my neck in a split second, squeezing the diamond collar into my skin. "You're his whore, and when I buy you from him, you'll be *my* whore. Or maybe when he's tired of your cunt, he'll just hand you over for free."

I grab his wrist and try to pry him away. "Let me go!"

Next thing I know, he's flying off me, and for a moment, I think it was me who sent him soaring through the air. That is, until I see Arran standing over him, his face contorted with fury.

"What the fuck was that for?" Landon demands, wiping blood off his bottom lip. "Fucking asshole."

"Skye, go to the bedroom and shut the door," he orders.

My heart jumps into my throat as I glance between the two brothers. One wearing a mask of primal rage. The other staring up at him in confusion.

Arran said he'd carve out the eyes of any man who saw me naked. But what would he do to one who touched me?

"What? Why? What are you going to do?"

"Go up. Now."

Oh my God, he's going to die. Arran is going to kill his own brother if I don't do something.

"Arran, please don't hurt him," I plead for the jerk. "Look at him. He's so scared. Just tell him to leave."

Arran swivels his head slowly toward me. "If you don't want him to die, do as I say."

"What the fuck is your problem?" I hear Landon ask as I scuttle away.

"My problem is, you touched what belongs to me."

10

ARRAN

He made his bed. Let him lie in it. Don't pay for his sins.
G. Black.

Although I tossed the note that arrived at my house this morning, I can still see it in my mind. The neat handwriting on vellum. Fancy prick.

But it's not the note itself that bothers me. It's that it was hand delivered to my front door. That I was in the house, getting ready for work, while he was right downstairs.

"He pulled up in a black Bentley. Said he was your friend and you were expecting this," Charles said when he gave it to me. "I asked if he wanted to wait for you to come downstairs, but he said he'd catch up with you later."

It's nothing but a scare tactic. He can't move into my home the way he took up residence in Noah Esposito's building. But he wants me to know that he can get to me whenever he wants.

"Arran?"

I sit up and smile. "It's me, Father."

Looking confused, he frowns. "I thought you left hours ago."

"Well, I've only been here for a few minutes."

His brows lift and he looks at the digital clock on the nightstand. "It's so hard to tell what time it is with no windows."

"It's for your own safety. As soon as the danger passes, you can go home."

He's trembling uncontrollably and struggles to get himself to the edge of the bed he's lying on. I quickly go to assist him, but he swats at my hands.

"I can do it," he argues but falls back onto the pillow.

The irony of the situation doesn't escape me. He's certainly made his bed in many ways, and he's lying in it. But that doesn't mean I'm going to let Gideon Black kill him.

Finally, after several tries, he manages to sit. A long sigh escapes him, sounding a lot like a haunted sob. "Ah, Arran. I can't today with you. Leave me alone."

There's a soft knock, followed by the sound of the electronic locking mechanism disengaging. Martha, Father's aid, enters carrying a tray with juice and medicines.

"Arran," she greets. "Didn't expect to see you until later."

"I have something to discuss with Father."

"Mmm." She sets down the tray on the nightstand. "Today might not be the best day. He didn't sleep well."

Father rubs his eyes. "It's that shit you give me," he tells her. "I need something stronger. Something that will keep the nightmares away."

"Clive, I've told you, it's those meds that got you into trouble in the first place. What you need is therapy." She gives me a meaningful glance.

"He'll return to his usual routines soon," I assure her. "This is only temporary."

"Don't you have a therapist you can trust to come here?" she asks.

"Arran doesn't even trust you," Father scoffs. "That's why he's keeping you prisoner, like me."

Martha purses her lips. "Prisoner, my ass. I can leave anytime I want." She hands him his drink and a small dose of his drug of choice.

"Then why don't you leave?" He downs the pills with a desperation that irks me. If I could toss those things down the toilet and keep him from ever taking them again without consequence, I would. But I learned the hard way that that's a mistake. "If I could get out of this hellhole, I'd be gone by now."

"Because he's paying me!" she replies. "Now, I'll be back in an hour with your lunch. Maybe we can watch a movie. Sound good?"

He huffs and she waves a dismissive hand as she leaves. "Always so ornery."

Father is wrong. I do trust her. She's been with us for too long not to. Martha was hired on as our nanny when we were children. Later on, she became the majordomo at our house. After Kate's death, when Father fell into his addiction and became ill, it was she who took care of him. Not our mother, who couldn't stand him when she was married to him, much less now. Not even his current wife, Kelly, who used his last affair as an excuse to go gallivanting somewhere in Spain, and we prefer her gone. It was always Martha.

"Let me go too," Father pleads.

"And be on the run for the rest of your life?" I ask.

"Gideon Black is out for blood. Your blood. You remember I told you about Stephen's son, don't you?"

His stare goes blank, the way it always does when I ask about Stephen Black. I know he hears me but doesn't want to answer questions about his involvement in his death.

"Father," I urge. "Do you remember Stephen? Is there anything you can tell me that would help?"

"What does it matter? I want to die." There's so much sadness in his tone, it touches me in spite of my determination to remain strict with him. "I want to see Kate."

I sit back in the chair and look at him thoughtfully, swallowing down the pain his words cause. "He won't stop at your death. He'll come after Landon when he inherits Maxton Holdings."

"What?"

"That's Gideon's game. He doesn't only want the men responsible for his father's death. He wants to make sure their families lose all power."

"But Landon is no threat." His facial features begin to relax as his medication takes effect. "You're more of a threat than he is. If Gideon Black is smart, he'll figure that out."

My brow furrows as I consider what he's just said. It's a confirmation of what I've suspected since the first message the Ferryman sent me.

"I've been receiving letters from him," I say. "He wants me to turn you over to him in exchange for my life."

When my father doesn't reply, I glance up to find him gone, his gaze glassy as he stares at me. Through me. "Kate," he whispers. "I need you to know, Kate."

I roll my hands into fists. "Kate isn't here, Father. She died, remember?"

He blinks at me, forcing tears from his eyes. "Bring me Kate, please. Arran. Bring Kate. I must speak with her."

Sheer frustration fills me, and I leave him crying out for my sister. Making me feel as helpless as the day she was murdered.

———

After the visit with my father, I attempt to work. I go to the Maxton corporate office and sit in front of my laptop with the intent of catching up on emails and calls. But I can't shake off the overwhelming darkness looming over me.

It's like this every time I visit him, which is why I usually go in the evenings. The blame for my mistake can be placed solely on a certain gray-eyed beauty waiting for me at home. I went before noon because I wanted Father to give me a sense of absolution for keeping Skye. I went to tell him that I have Thomas Cameron's daughter. That she belongs to me and that, even in the grave, I can make him pay through her.

It was supposed to give him a sense of closure.

But I didn't say a word for the same reason that I never told him that it was me who ordered the hit. Because when he learned of what I'd done to Yegor, he begged me not to touch Thomas. He made me swear.

"Please, Arran. No more bloodshed. Swear to me that you will not hurt him," Father pleaded. "Kate would be ashamed."

I swore to him that I would not touch Thomas. Instead, I called in the favor Noah Esposito owed me. That was what the agreement was, that I'd give him the name of one of Maxton House's clients, a list I keep very private. In exchange, he'd do a hit for me. No questions asked.

At first, he was reluctant. It seems the hitman-turned-Don of the Gianni family has morals.

"I don't want innocent blood on my hands," he'd said to me.

"There won't be. Thomas Cameron is anything but innocent and he deserves to burn in hell for what he did. I want you to send him there."

Then I told him everything, and, in the end, he agreed. He followed him to Louda Underground Lounge and took him out in the bathroom, leaving him half naked with his head in the urinal. He was shamed, humiliated after death, just as my sister had been.

Father heard of the death, of course, and was horrified by it. How could anyone be capable of such a thing?

He'll never know I was behind it. That *I* am capable of it and so much more. For Kate.

If Father was opposed to the judge being hurt, he would certainly be opposed to the things I'm doing with Skye. He'd demand I let her go, make me promise to. And that's something I'm not prepared to do.

Fuck no. There's no way in hell I'm letting her go now. Not when her scent still clings to me. Not when I can close my eyes and conjure up the way her skin feels against mine. The way she tastes. Not when I haven't been inside her yet.

Blood flows to my dick at the mere idea of her, and I curse myself for having taken Wesley's bait. He knew I'd pay a much higher price than anyone else. Now he has one million dollars of my money and I have a fucking perpetual hard-on for my enemy's daughter.

"Fuck me. Devon!"

"Sir?" Devon pokes his head into the office.

I'm already up and collecting my things. "Cancel any meetings I might have for the rest of the day and tomorrow."

"Even the Williams meeting? They were expecting the proposal for their return on the fifty loans."

"Fuck." I grind my teeth in annoyance. Michael Williams is Maxton Holdings' largest client during the day, investing millions with us. At night, he's one of the wealthiest guests at Maxton House.

"Change the meeting to Maxton House Saturday night. Tell him he'll be a guest at my table *and* I'll zero out the auction house fees on anything he wants."

Devon's eyes widen because he knows that some of those fees can be staggering, depending on the item. "Yes, sir."

Shit. That pussy is going to cost me more than one million. I pinch the bridge of my nose. "Thank you, Dev."

He makes to leave but turns back. "Oh, Lilly's Den called. They have the order ready and asked if you wish for them to deliver it."

"No. I'll pick it up on the way home."

I leave though I shouldn't, lured back to Skye and her soft skin and sweet pussy. My jaw hurts from the tension caused by the constant battle between my desire and hatred for her. But both urge me to return to her side, to pull her against me. To taste her again and make her come.

My hand begins to shake as my driver seems to take the longest route to Lilly's Den, like a fucking drug addict aware that a fix is just around the corner but still so far out of reach.

"Frank," I grit through my teeth. "Can't you drive faster?"

"Driving faster only takes you to an early grave. Is that what you want, boss?"

I grumble my response so as not to disrespect my elder. The moment the car stops in front of the shop, I rush out to get the items I ordered this morning. I'm back in the vehicle within minutes. "Let's go."

"She must be some girl." His gaze meets mine through the rearview mirror and he laughs. "I've never seen you this eager."

I don't justify his stupid remark with an answer. Instead, I pick up the call that's coming in to my cell phone. It's from my doorman.

"What is it, Charles?"

"Landon is here," he says. "I told him you were at the office, but he insisted on waiting for you in the house."

"Motherfucker." I clutch the phone hard to keep myself from throwing it out the window. "What the fuck is he doing there?"

"He just said he needs to speak with you."

I can't legally keep him out of the house, not when it's under Father's name. But Landon stopped showing up unannounced when I removed any and all important documents. There's nothing of value for him to swipe.

Except there is.

"Charles, get in that house and find Miss Cameron. Escort her to my suite upstairs."

"Shit!" He curses and I hear what sounds like rattling and the other men whispering. "He's set the inside lock."

"I'm less than two minutes away, but keep trying."

I open up the app that connects me to the cameras in the house and go room to room in search of my brother. When I find him, the desire to kill something fills my veins, heating my blood to nearly a boil.

He's in the study at the liquor cabinet. Though I can't hear what he's saying, I can tell he's speaking. I tweak the camera in the direction Landon is staring to find Skye cautiously moving around my desk.

The doe eyes she used with me are gone. In their place is a narrowed gaze. Her body language doesn't scream fear but distrust.

Then, to my surprise, she smiles and says something, right before she makes a beeline for the door.

In two strides, he reaches her, grabs her by the arm, and drags her back inside. My vision goes red as I watch him press her against the wall and insinuate his leg between hers.

"Frank, step on that fucking gas," I order.

We arrive at the house a minute later. I throw the door open before the car has come to a complete stop. When I enter the vestibule, Charles is pounding on the door while another one of my security detail is working to pick the lock.

I have the key already in hand and before anyone can greet me, I'm storming through the foyer toward the study, my ears pounding and my skin on fire.

"I'm not a whore." I hear her say.

They come into view and what I see spins me into another level of rage.

His fingers around her neck, his teeth bared and so close to her face. "You're his whore, and when I buy you from him, you'll be my whore. Or maybe when he's tired of your cunt, he'll just hand you over for free."

"Let me go!" she cries.

I barely register his weight as I haul him off her and throw him across the room. Then I'm on him, my fist making contact with his chin once before I regain some semblance of control and stand.

"What the fuck was that for?" Landon demands, wiping blood off his bottom lip. "Fucking asshole."

I can barely breathe or think beyond the fact that

Landon had his hands on her. "Skye, go to the bedroom and shut the door."

"What? Why? What are you going to do?"

If I could, I'd tear him apart. Who knows? If he provokes me enough, I still might. "Go up. Now," I repeat.

But she doesn't listen. Instead, she seems to feel sorry for him. "Arran, please don't hurt him. Look at him. He's so scared. Just tell him to leave."

With utter disbelief, I turn to the woman. "If you don't want him to die, do as I say."

"What the fuck is your problem?" Landon demands.

I turn back to him. "My problem is, you touched what belongs to me."

11

ARRAN

I narrow my eyes at my older brother. He's sitting across the desk from me, tending to his swelling lip with the towel and bag of ice I threw at him a few minutes earlier.

"Stop fucking glaring at me like I ate the last piece of your pie. She's fine. I barely even touched her."

A growl escapes me. "The key word being *barely*. Which means you did."

He lifts his gaze to me. "What the fuck does it matter? She's just a thing you bought."

I lean back and steeple my fingers beneath my chin. Were he any other man, I would have killed him. Though for the life of me, I don't know why seeing his hands on her infuriates me. I've never wanted to kill anyone who's touched a woman I've been with before. Perhaps it's that I do actually see her as mine. Completely and utterly mine.

"It matters," I tell him. "Skye is off limits to you and anyone else. Is that clear?"

"You know that I own all of this shit, don't you? That money you bought her with, it's mine," he hisses.

I chuckle, low and menacingly. "Your fucking money, is it? You would think that."

"It's true. My name is on everything. Including this house."

My eye twitches. "Let me make something clear. The money I use is mine and no one else's. Not yours. Not Father's. As for the buildings, Father owns them. Which means you don't have shit."

He grins. "For now. But eventually, it will all be mine. Don't go believing what everyone says about you being his true heir. All that matters legally is that my name is on that fucking will."

"Have you ever asked yourself why that is? Why I run the fucking company yet don't fight you inheriting it? Are you really so dense?"

The answer eludes him. I can tell the wheels in his head are spinning at full capacity, but he just can't put it together. Not that I lay the blame on him. While Mother kept him glued to her side, teaching him how to spend money and flaunt it, I remained with Father, learning how to make it. Learning how to be smart and savvy and fucking ruthless.

Yes, Landon will inherit the company and all the risks that come with it. I will retain control of the empire. He cannot remove me from my position without a hefty severance that could bankrupt the Maxton Corporation. And if the company fails, he takes the fall and I go free and clear.

Father has never outright told me why he updated his last will and testament to read this way. It was shortly after Kate died, and though the drugs hadn't fully taken effect, he was in deep mourning. Not that he's ever managed to get out of it.

I'm not sure, but I think he did it for Mother's benefit so

that she'd stop harassing him over giving Landon more since he's the eldest. A way to give her what she wanted, without actually giving it to her.

Father cares for Landon. But there's no doubt he sees him as Mother's son more than his own.

Suddenly, I see Landon in a different light. He's weak and vulnerable and doesn't even know it.

All of my fury deflates. "What are you doing here, Landon?"

Smiling, he gently touches his puffy lip. "I heard about your little purchase and wanted to confirm for myself that it was true."

Frowning, I ask, "Where did you hear about it?"

He shrugs. "I have ways."

"You mean you're spying on me," I state.

"I mean gossip always has a way of moving fast through certain circles."

"Well, now you've seen for yourself that it's true."

He studies me with that ever-present fool's grin. "What made you do it? She's insanely hot, but didn't you think her daddy"—he draws a line across his throat and drops his head to the side, his tongue hanging out—"offed Kate."

And this is why I hate my own brother. Why I'll never confide in him that it was me who had Thomas killed or the real reason I have Skye in my home.

"That's in the past," I say. "Thomas is dead now anyway. And like you said, she's insanely hot."

"So, how is she?" He waggles his brows and my scowl deepens. "She looks like she's a hellcat in bed."

"Landon," I say, pinching the bridge of my nose the way I tend to do when something really annoys me. "I have a lot on my plate today. If that was all you needed—"

"Actually, there is something else." He sits up and lifts

his hand to me, displaying the Maxton House ring on his finger. "I want to take a couple of friends to the auction Saturday and need you to add them to the guest list."

"You want to take a couple of friends to Maxton House," I repeat. "It isn't some fucking bar you take a couple of friends to for drinks."

"Yet somehow, that's exactly what I'm going to do." Landon leans back in his chair with his hands locked behind his head and gives me a condescending smirk.

"Fine. But do it next week. This weekend, I have an important client and I can't have your drunk frat boys to worry about."

"Frat boys." He laughs. "We're not in university anymore."

"Yet somehow, that's exactly what you behave like," I say, borrowing his words. "Next week. If you must intrude into our business, do it then."

"This Saturday." He leans forward, doing his best to appear threatening. "Don't forget, little brother, I can come with or without your permission. But I'd rather not cause a scene."

The throbbing at my temples that always accompanies Landon begins to form. I clench my jaw, partly from the tension caused by the fury his threat evokes.

"Fine," I say. "But you'll follow the rules. The second they get rowdy, they're out. And I won't give a fuck about scenes."

"You won't even know we're there." As he stands, he makes a waving motion with both hands, the kind a magician does after a disappearing act. "See you later, little brother."

"Landon." I stop him before he exits. "Have you received any threatening letters?"

"Why the fuck would anyone threaten *me*?" He salutes me and leaves.

The better question is, why *not* him?

———

When I step into my bedroom, I find Skye staring out the window, her arms crossed over her chest. "You didn't carve his eyes out."

I smirk. "Not yet."

She peeks over her shoulder at me, then turns fully, her gaze following me as I move to the leather chair across from the bed. I unzip my pants and release my already hard cock before I sit.

"Come," I say to her.

She obeys like I knew she would, stopping right in front of me.

The thing is, just because I didn't hurt Landon doesn't mean I was able to shake off the aggression. My nerves still tense when I recall the image of his hand on her.

He touched what's mine and I have the sudden urge to wipe her skin of him.

"Take off your clothes." My tone is low and steady but demanding.

Again, she obeys without hesitation, removing everything but the diamond collar.

"Straddle me."

Swallowing hard, she places one knee on the chair, then the other. She steadies herself with her hands on my shoulders as she lowers her ass onto the top of my legs.

Her lovely tits hang round and full in front of me, her dark nipples pert, ready to be sucked. I let my gaze drop further down, to where her pussy is spread open, exposing her delicious little clit.

A smile paints across my lips. "Make yourself come on my dick, Skye."

"What?"

"Rub yourself on me until you come. I want my dick slick with your juices."

Chewing on her lower lip, she looks between us, her sweet cunt just an inch from my dick. She lifts herself slightly and grazes my shaft with her clit, from balls to tip and back.

She does it again and again, each time, pressing herself more against me, until she's grinding into me hard. Her wetness spreads over the length of me, coating me, making me slick for her.

Taking her right nipple between my teeth, I bite down until she hisses. I suck the pebbled peak into my mouth, circle it with my tongue, and bite again.

When I have her panting, I move to the left one. The more sensitive one. As I expected, she cries out, thrusting her chest forward.

"Bite harder," she begs, then moans when I comply. Her body heat rises as do the sounds of her moans. She's getting herself off on me, pumping her hips over me, just the way I wanted her to.

I alternate between licking her nipples and trailing my tongue over her clavicle, biting the spot at the crook of her neck. The scent of her arousal and the feel of her burning flesh is enough to make me come, but I refuse to let go. Not yet. Not until I hear her screaming.

And she's so close, her fingernails digging into my shoulders, her tempo increasing.

Then she tries to kiss me, and I grasp her arms to hold her back. "Unless you're ready to get fucked right here and now, don't. Whether you ask for it or not, I'll fuck you if you kiss me."

The haze seems to clear momentarily, and her motions slow long enough to ask, "You'd rape me?"

"You've been warned. If you kiss me, you better mean it, because I'll lose control. I'll fuck you, Skye." Fuck, as it is, I'm barely hanging on by a thread. If her tongue slides across mine, I won't care about anything but being inside her.

Her eyes bore into me for a second before she's grinding herself harder than ever. She cries out and throws her head back, her movements jerky as she comes.

Panting, she slumps against my chest. I give her only a short respite.

"Skye."

"Mmm." She sighs.

"You made a mess on me."

"Mmm."

"Clean it."

At my tone, she lifts her face. "I'll get a towel," she says.

But when she tries to get up, I snatch her by the wrist and haul her down. "With your mouth."

Something strange passes over her gaze. Then she drops to her knees on the floor and places herself comfortably between my legs. Almost reverently, she wraps her small hand around my dick and looks at it, her beautiful gray eyes filling with lust again.

"I've never tasted myself before," she says.

"You've been missing out, because you're fucking delicious."

A smile appears on her lips as she pumps her hand up

and down until a drop of pre-cum forms on the tip. "I have a feeling a dash of this will make it even better."

I'm left speechless and dumb as she takes me between those plump lips and sucks. I don't know what my intention was when I asked her to clean me off. Part of it was to shock her. Remind her that, no matter what, she's mine. A greater part just wanted her to suck my dick.

I certainly didn't intend on her knocking the wind out of me with her sexy fucking words and the hunger with which she's doing it. Like she can't get enough.

She swirls her tongue over the tip of my cock, one hand at the base because I'm too big for her to take me fully, the other grazing my balls with her fingernails. Then she pushes down so that the head slides all the way to her throat, where she moans and the vibrations travel like electricity through my entire body.

"Fuck, Skye," I groan, thrusting my fingers into her thick waves and guiding her up and down. "You feel so good."

Up and down she moves, and all the while, her eyes remain on mine. And they touch me in a completely different way.

She is so fucking beautiful, looking at me as I fuck her mouth. As I shove my cock again and again past those full pink lips.

"Drink me, Skye. Every fucking drop." I fist her hair and I begin to thrust deeper, hitting the back of her throat, then I come.

Not once does she pull away, swallowing all I have to give.

When the spasms end, I release my hold on her hair and she sits back on her haunches. Inspecting her work as she wipes the corner of her mouth with her thumb, she says, "Squeaky clean."

"Shit."

She grins, a wicked, knowing sort of smile that fades when I reach out and trace her collar. "I have to shower," she growls. "Suddenly, I feel dirty."

Pushing away, she leaves me to stare after her. I don't follow her, because I can't move. And I don't say anything, because I'm not sure what the fuck has pissed her off.

Luckily, the shower seems to calm her, and when she comes out wrapped in a towel, she looks to be in a better mood. "What's that?"

"Some things I ordered for you," I tell her as I set everything on the bed.

Coming to stand beside me, she touches the embossed name on one of five black boxes. "Lilly's Den, Arran, that place is very expensive."

"Lilly is a friend of my mother's."

"So she charges you less?"

My lips pull down. "I have no idea."

A small giggle escapes her. "You're definitely rich. God, I used to love going there. But I could only get myself one thing at a time."

"Aren't you going to see what's inside?"

With a slight tilt of her head, as if she's afraid there's a bomb in it, she lifts the top off the smallest box. From it, she pulls out several pieces of lacy and silky lingerie.

Curiously, I reach in too and hook my finger through a thong. Instantly, I envision this scrap of fabric tucked intimately against Skye's sweet cunt.

"I hope this bra fits. Usually, I have a hard time because my boobs are—" She cuts off when she glances at me. "What are you doing?"

Behind the thong pressed to my mouth, I smile. "Planning."

She rolls her eyes and proceeds to open another box. "Ooh, Arran, look." With excitement, she takes out three pairs of stretch pants and matching tank tops. Grabbing one, she rubs it on her cheek. "They're so soft."

Then she tears through the rest, finding an assortment of clothes for different occasions, just as I requested— shorts, shirts, socks, pants, and even a coat.

"Last one," she says, going for the last package. Biting her lower lip, she lifts the top and sets it aside.

Her big gray eyes go wide as she peers at the shimmery black material. "It's a gown." She gets it and goes to the mirror. Holding it against her, she looks at herself from different angles. "Arran, it's gorgeous."

"I'm glad you like it."

"Did you choose it?" she asks. "I ask because it's going to be revealing with that deep plunge. I'd hate for your jealousy to show." She winks at me mischievously through her reflection. "Although the cut is so classic."

"We're going to the Maxton Auction House Saturday night. It will be appropriate."

"Maxton Auction House?" She seems confused. "Do you mean Asta?"

"No. Maxton House auctions off items like art, furniture. Things, not people."

"I've never heard of it." Her brows pinch together as if she's searching her memory for mention of it.

"It's black market."

Shaking her head, she says, "Why am I not surprised."

"Well, are you going to try it on? I want to see you in that gown."

Her lips tug slightly upward as she releases the towel

and lets it drop in a puddle at her feet.

My eyes trail up her beautiful long legs to the sweetness between them. "Maybe I'd rather you stay this way."

"And miss an opportunity to torture you a little? Never."

She slips into the long, formfitting silver dress with the plunging neckline I wasn't thrilled with, but it's sheer perfection on Skye. She's statuesque and beautiful. A starlet from the golden age.

"You look lovely," I say.

"I'm thinking I should leave my hair down. Or up? Down." She grabs her long tresses and lifts them, drops them, then lifts them again as she examines herself.

Going to her, I whisper near her ear, "Down."

She turns to me. "Thank you for the clothes."

"You're welcome."

Then she reaches for her collar's clasp and undoes it.

Before she can drag the thing off her neck, I grab hold of her hands. "That belongs on you."

"But..." she begins, and the confusion in her gaze is clear. "I'm not wearing it with the dress. Everyone will know that—"

"You belong to me," I finish for her. "You do." Stepping closer, I lean in so that my nose is in her hair. "Never take it off, Skye. As long as you belong to me, you will wear that collar."

"Like a dog," she hisses. "Will I wear a leash too?"

"Skye!"

Biting back whatever retort she has, she looks away. I can tell she's fighting to keep her mouth shut, and in the end, she loses.

"You like owning me too much."

A grin I hope reminds her of who I am spreads over my lips. "I don't just like it. I love it."

12

MAISIE

I'm in my room—or as much as anyone being held against their will can consider a room theirs—sitting in bed, flipping through the pages of my sketchbook.

The very first drawing is called *Justice Girl*. She's a police officer who turns vigilante when her partner is killed in action. For years, she's invincible, taking down criminals by breaking some laws herself.

Even though the book is full with my creations, she's my favorite. Probably because I didn't exactly create her. She already existed.

"Momma," I whisper as I trail my fingertip over the sketch. "I miss you."

"What are you doing?" I look up to find Scarlet leaning against the doorjamb.

"Nothing."

She frowns. "Thinking up new cartoons to draw?"

"They're comics," I remind her. "And no. There are no blank pages left." I shut the book and toss it across the bed with a loud sigh.

"Hmm. Well, I'm going to take a shower. Afterward, we can order something to eat."

"Whatever," I say and wait for her to leave.

When her footsteps disappear, I grab the sketchbook again. I flip it open to Rage. Damn, Scarlet seriously reminds me of her. A part of me feels like maybe she's Rage come to life.

But Mom and Scarlet aren't the only ones my characters resemble. I turn to one of the last pages, until I come to *Hacker*. She's a feisty teen who can hack into any system. There's no firewall too high, no password too unique that can keep her out.

A plan begins to form in my head, one I don't really have time to think over too much. I leave my room and go down the hall, pausing at Scarlet's suite.

I peek inside. Beyond the bed is the door to her bathroom. It's slightly ajar, but I can't see through the crack.

Moving as quiet as a mouse, needing to be sure she's in there, I step close enough to see her through the reflection in the mirror above the sink. She bends out of sight, turns on the shower, and when she comes into view again, she's taken off her long-sleeve turtleneck. I slap a hand over my mouth to stifle a gasp at the horror of what I see.

Dozens of thin scars cover her back, from her shoulders all the way down to her waist. Zigzagging lines that have no rhyme or reason.

She gets into the tub and pulls the shower curtain closed. I blink several times, trying to get the image out of my head. Was she in an accident? Or worse, was she whipped?

I shove all those thoughts out of my mind and leave the room.

Down the hall, right before the kitchen, is Scarlet's office. I'm sure if she had any idea of what I can do, she would have locked the door. Or, at the very least, secured her computer.

Sliding into the chair, I open the laptop and go to work. It's not that hard to get in if you know how to bypass certain login screens. Which I do.

"Sorry, Momma," I say, glancing upward. She's probably looking down from Heaven with disappointment. Although Daddy did always say that Skye needed to go into law so she could keep me out of jail, my mom was probably hoping that wouldn't actually happen.

"That is the sort of thing I arrested people for, Maze," I can almost hear her say. "We must abide by the law if we want others to follow."

Doing what's right is what got her killed. That thought has me pausing, my finger over the Return key.

I don't want to disappoint Momma. But I also don't want to die.

I hit the key, and I'm in. Windows pop up as the screen fills with whatever applications were being used before it was shut down.

The last to load are a set of PDFs. I'm about to click out of them so that I can search files when I catch a glimpse of what they are. Newspaper articles from November of 2004. But it's not the date that has my attention. It's the photograph of a little girl.

Eight-year-old Tamberleigh Johnson was found wandering the streets of Jackson after her parents, Travis and Elaine Johnson, were brutally killed just outside the city. It is believed that the young girl was witness to the murder, and she's been taken into protective custody.

Leaning in, I get a better look at her. She has curly

blonde hair and chubby cheeks and could be anyone. But her green eyes tell me who she really is. Scarlet.

"Take your fingers off the keys." There's a click before she presses something hard to the back of my head.

I instantly lift my hands. "Don't shoot. I didn't see anything."

"Liar." She reaches around me and slams the laptop shut. "Get up."

"I can explain."

"Scoot!" If her tone isn't enough to make me move, her digging the barrel of her gun into my skull does the trick. "Sit," she orders when I go around the desk.

I do as she says, plopping my ass down in the chair. That's when I get a glimpse of what she's holding. "You've got to be kidding me. A stapler? You threatened me with a freaking stapler?"

"You'd be surprised what I can do with this. And don't cuss."

"Freaking isn't a cuss word. Fucking is." I cross my arms over my chest and huff. "Of course you wouldn't threaten me for real. Giddy needs me alive."

"Kid, you keep calling him that and he *is* going to want you dead." She leans against the desk and scrutinizes me. I scrutinize her back.

Her hair is dripping water onto her shirt and she's got a towel wrapped around her waist, as if she ran out of the shower in a hurry and didn't have time to put pants on. She's tapping her foot in that way Daddy used to do when I'd get in trouble and he couldn't figure out what to do with me.

"How the hell did you get into my computer anyway?" she asks.

I shrug. "I'm a genius."

Smirking, she says, "What you are is a handful."

"So I've been told."

"Where did you learn to hack?"

"The internet." It's amazing the things you can learn by doing a simple search.

Scarlet shakes her head. "What were you looking for? Maisie?" she prompts when it takes me too long to answer.

"I don't know. Anything that will help Skye and me," I admit.

"The only thing that will help you two is your sister getting the location on Clive Maxton."

Suddenly, the helplessness of my situation hits me like a pile of bricks to the chest. I turn away from her before she can see the tears that prick at my eyes. I hate it when people see me weep.

"Ah, shit. Are you crying?"

"No," I sob.

"Don't cry." She pats my head and I glare at her. "Sorry. I'm not good at comforting and I really would rather you stopped. It makes me uncomfortable."

"I just..." I wipe my cheeks. "I don't want to just sit here and literally wait to be rescued. I'm powerless!"

Sighing, Scarlet rubs her temples. Then she goes around her desk and, from a bottom drawer, produces a Chromebook. Setting it down, she pushes it toward me.

I take it. "What's this for?"

"It's obvious you're good with computers. See if you can come up with something on Clive or Arran Maxton. Something we haven't thought of."

My brows shoot upward in surprise. "Are you serious?"

Nodding, she says, "You need something to keep you busy. And you're not powerless, Maisie. If you were, Gideon wouldn't have left you with me."

I bite back a proud smile. "Thanks."

"You're welcome."

She makes to leave, but I stop her. "Scarlet."

Pausing at the door, she looks over her shoulder at me. "Yeah?"

"That family in the article... Was that your family?"

Her hands roll into fists at her sides. "If you ever try to break into my personal things again, I'll kill you."

I recoil from her words and something in her expression shifts. Like she doesn't know what to do.

She drops her gaze to the floor and bites her lower lip as if she's mulling something over. "Come."

"Where?"

"I know what it's like to feel like a helpless kid. I'm going to make sure that doesn't happen to you."

13

SKYE

I've been here three days now, and, still, not a single clue as to where Clive Maxton could be hiding. And I've searched every day to the best of my ability. Arran leaves. I explore.

If he's seen any of it through the many cameras he claims there are, nothing's been mentioned. Or maybe he's not even watching me at all because he's that sure there's nothing to find.

"How long will you be today?" I ask him, waiting lazily in bed as he gets dressed.

"Only a few hours. I'm going to check on some of my other businesses, then straight back." He wraps a gold-colored tie around his neck and begins to work on the knot.

Fuck me, there's just something about him that draws me in, and I can't stop staring. What is it about a man putting on a tie that's so sexy? Or is it just him?

I flip onto my back and peer at the ceiling, hating that I like anything about him. "You have other businesses?"

"Investing in different companies is smart. If one goes down, you always have a source of income."

"That is smart," I say more to myself than him.

He appears in my peripheral, looking at me like I'm a juicy piece of steak. "I have to go." He tugs the blanket down to my knees, and his gaze darkens several shades. "There's no time for breakfast now, but when I come home, I want you in my mouth."

With the tip of his finger, he traces the line of my pussy as he bends down to suck on a nipple. I inhale sharply as he teases me, knowing full well that he's going to get me hot and wet.

But that's his point. To leave me in a tortured state. Something he confirms when he orders in a deep, commanding tone, "Do not touch yourself. I'll know it if you do. When I get home, you're going to come on my tongue."

I nod, unable to speak through my dry mouth.

It takes me a while to calm enough to get out of bed. When I do, it's straight to the shower. The water is already warm when I turn on the faucet, and steam instantly builds. I step inside, letting the hot jets hit my back, and I'm greeted by the sight of the happy orchids. Arran cared for them this morning. All of the dead parts have been snipped away, and they've even been rotated and moved closer to the window.

Strange man. Ruthless and cruel yet has the capability of being caring and gentle.

Ugh. That drives me insane. It would be so much easier if he were awful all the way around. If he didn't love his sister so fiercely or care for delicate flowers or buy me nice clothes. If he didn't make me burn like a wick doused in lighter fluid.

When I get home, you're going to come on my tongue.

Wishing I could scrape the sound of his words out of my

head, I scrub my scalp extra hard. It doesn't work. But the temptation of playing with myself isn't even there, not when I know he'll return soon enough, and then he'll torture me the way that makes me a greater slave to him than anything else.

I should be ashamed, wanting the enemy like I do. Daddy probably really *is* rolling in his grave—as Arran intends every time he touches me—horrified that his own daughter is betraying him over and over again.

I dress in a pink cotton shirt and blue knee-length skirt and am heading downstairs when, suddenly, I get the urge to run. To break out of this prison and go as hard and fast as I can. See how far I can get without getting a bullet to the back of my head.

The front door looms ahead of me as I reach the bottom of the stairs. It wouldn't be so difficult to leave. Arran said I could anytime I chose. His guards won't stop me. The prison walls are of my own making, after all.

Before I know what I'm doing, I'm at the door, turning the knob and pulling. Charles, who's sitting at the long desk along with two other men, glances up at me from his cell phone.

"Good morning, Miss Cameron."

I step into the vestibule with them. They all watch me with friendly smiles. "Good morning." I move farther, to the door that leads straight onto Delancey Street. Swallowing nervously, I grab the handle but don't pull.

"Can I help you with anything?" Charles asks.

"I... I was thinking of taking a walk," I say.

He remains silent for a moment, then adds, "They're calling for some nasty weather. It might be dangerous to leave the house."

I look at the clear blue sky through one of the windows.

"Yes. Bad weather." Releasing the handle, I turn back to Charles. "But if I wanted to dance in the rain, would you let me?"

A soft smile tugs his lips. "Yes. But I'd give you an umbrella. You can dance in the rain if that's what you want to do."

Sighing, I nod and make my way back into the house and shut the door quietly behind me.

So it's true, then. I'm the only thing standing between me and my enemies. Those who might be aware I'm here, anyway. Charles would have let me go. But he would have sent me armed.

The unexpected kindness makes me smile. Even amongst thieves, there is honor.

———

Cooking has always been something I take great pleasure in. Not the act of it necessarily, but the memories it brings. Momma was a full-time officer at the Philadelphia Police Department. Once she was promoted to lead detective, it became even harder for her to spend time with her girls.

To make the most out of every minute with us, she insisted that we cook at least one meal together. Maisie despised cooking, so she'd usually disappear halfway through. But I found it soothing to learn her traditional Scottish recipes, her telling me about her youth while I spilled all of my teen woes on her shoulder.

I miss my mother. Desperately wish she were here so that I could tell her about Daddy and Arran and all of the ways I feel like a fucked-up mess.

How I'm so full of fear that were it not for Maisie, I'd be frozen by it.

So I go to the kitchen and search for something to make. Arran isn't Scottish. Actually, I'm not exactly sure what he is. Regardless, there's very little in his pantry that resembles the fully stocked one Momma kept.

"Cooking is cooking." I decide to make fully loaded omelets. Anything that can bring me that sense of connection with my mother. Where even if I can't speak with her, she might hear me calling.

I cut peppers, onions, and mushrooms, grate a block of gruyere cheese, and blister grape tomatoes. There's a loaf of fresh bread, and I slather it with butter, then toss it in the oven.

I'm so focused that I don't notice the passing of time. Thoughts of everything that's happened are placed on the back burner. All that matters is the crafting of this delicious meal.

That is, until I catch sight of something in my peripheral. A slightly raised panel in the butler's pantry, which is located between the kitchen and formal dining room. Narrowing my gaze, I approach it and run my fingertips over the edge.

I hadn't noticed this before, and I've searched everything, including the liquor cabinet in this area. That means, at one point, this panel was flush with the wall and invisible.

Pulling it, I manage to open what I now realize is a door. Before me is a narrow wooden staircase leading to the basement. I hit the light switch just inside, and the space illuminates brightly.

"Hello!" I call down.

Biting my lower lip, I take one step, then another. Above me, I hear the door softly close again. Arran did say I could go anywhere I want to. If he catches me down here, he can't be upset about it.

"Hello," I call again, just in case.

When I reach the bottom of the stairs, I get a good view of just how large the basement is. It has to be even larger than the footprint of the house!

In one section, I pass furniture that's been covered with white sheets. "Those are gonna get musty," I say to myself.

Farther in are shelves full of dishes and glassware, perhaps saved for dinner parties. There are also large quantities of supplies—canned foods, bottled water, and paper goods.

I duck under pipes and go around cement pilings until I get to a small wine cellar. Must be some expensive shit in there, because there's an iron door with a huge lock.

Besides all of that, there isn't much else. No boxes to snoop through or bodies to discover. Just me, an old boiler, and a bunch of stuff I bet Arran doesn't even use.

"Well, that was a waste of—" There's a strange zapping sound at the same time that the lights above brighten, making me squint. Then it all goes pitch-black.

My eyes widen even though I can't see a single thing. Out of instinct, I spread my legs slightly and my arms go out, as if I'm on a tightrope and need to balance because I can no longer perceive the floor.

"Hello!" This time, when I call out, it's more of a plea. "Is anyone up there?"

I chastise myself for coming down here. Nothing good ever happens to anyone who goes into a basement. That's why they always put that in horror movies!

"Hello!"

Okay, Skye, deep breath. It's just a little darkness. You'll be fine. Just move slow and steady. Retrace your steps.

I begin to shuffle my feet forward, moving slowly and carefully. My head makes contact with the pipes above, and even in the dark, I see stars. "Shit!" I rub the sore spot.

Okay, go slower. Take your time. Start again.

Shuffle forward, feel around. Shuffle forward, feel around. So far, so good.

The temperature drops and I swear a little breeze tickles my face. Must be the airflow from the doorway.

Too confident, I move faster than I should. My foot catches on something, and just when I think I've managed to right myself, I kick my other foot and bang it full force against a hard object.

I go flying, and because I can't see, it seems like I'm airborne for a long time. My hands make first contact with one of the shelves. I try to grab on, but all I manage to do is push it so that both it and I crash hard onto the floor, and from the sound of shattering glass, I can tell it was all the dinner plates and glasses I passed earlier.

For a while, I stay down, breathing hard, assessing as much as possible the damage I've just inflicted upon myself. My palms and knees sting like hell, and if I'm not mistaken, I took a good hit to the ribs.

"Ouch." I move just a tad and glass crunches beneath me, imbedding itself into my knees. Out of all the days to wear a skirt, it had to be today.

I look upward. Or for all I know, it could be down. At this point, I'm not sure of anything.

"Help!" I cry, hoping one of the guards will hear me.

But what are the odds? There are two doors and a floor between us. I'm screwed.

Think, Skye, think. Unfortunately, all I can think about is the pain and the fact that nothing but willpower will get me out of this.

Ignoring the sting of glass sliding into my flesh, I push myself up. I remain still for a moment, catching my breath, wishing I could wipe away the wetness from my eyes—not that I'm crying, but it hurts like a bitch—yet afraid to accidentally put glass in them.

I try to find my way to the stairs again, this time much more carefully. Every inch I gain is agonizing, and all I can do is pray that my sense of direction doesn't lead me astray.

The next time I hit something, it's a step. I nearly slump with relief, but I'm so desperate to get the hell out of here, I don't allow myself the luxury.

Fast as I can, I rush up the stairs. But when I reach the top, it's only to find that the door has shut completely. I shove at it, pushing my shoulder against it with all my might. I even resort to slamming my injured palms against it.

"Shit!"

Now I do want to cry, and suddenly, the darkness isn't just darkness anymore. It's an all-consuming abyss of nothingness and I'm stuck in it all alone.

"Ahh!" I scream. "Fuck!"

I drop down onto the step and sulk. If God is real, he's either abandoned me or believes I can handle a lot more than I can and he's testing me.

Fuck it. It doesn't matter if I can handle it. I'm in this and don't have a choice.

Breathe. Just breathe.

Shutting my eyes against the oppressive lack of light, I press my back to the door and heave. Again and again, until I break out in a sweat.

Finally, I hear a click. Something gives, and the door swings open and I'm falling onto the floor at Arran's feet.

"Fuck!" I hear a second before I'm lifted. I barely have a

moment to get my bearings as he rushes to the kitchen with me in his arms. He sits me on the counter right next to the sink, then he's shuffling through drawers. "What did you fucking do? You're all fucked up, Skye!"

"I..." I peer down at my hands and legs and discover why he's so upset. "I fell."

From one of the drawers, he produces a white plastic box with a large red cross on it. He places it beside me and, with trembling hands, he searches through it.

"You fell? Down the stairs?" He grabs a piece of gauze and tweezers and begins to pluck the large pieces of glass from my knees. "Fuck, Skye. If I'd known you were this clumsy—"

"I'm not clum— Ouch!" I attempt to snatch the tweezers away. "I'll do it."

"The hell you will. Look at your hands. They're even worse than your knees. Fuck. Fuck. Fuck!"

"Why are you so angry? It's just a little blood." As I say it, a few drops get on his crisp white button-up shirt.

"I'm angry because it's *my* blood," he hisses.

I frown, but he seems so frustrated with me, I don't argue. Instead, I allow him to take care of the wounds. When he's fully cleaned my knees, he gets a roll of gauze and wraps them.

"Give me your hand." I do as he says, and he shakes his head. This time, it's with disappointment, and for some reason, that bothers me more.

"I'm not clumsy, I swear. It's just that the lights went out and it's pitch-black down there and the damned door closed."

"It's spring-loaded to keep it concealed."

"That's dangerous. Someone could get trapped down there," I add sarcastically.

"There's an emergency lever inside." He lifts his gaze to me. "What were you doing in the basement?"

I shrug a shoulder. "You said I could snoop."

Finishing with that hand, he wraps it too, then takes a hold of my left. "I've been having issues with the breakers down there. If you decide to go into areas that aren't part of the main house again, ask me. I'll come with you."

A burst of laughter bubbles from me. "You'll come with me while I snoop."

Tossing the last piece of glass into the sink, he begins to wrap the injury. "If you must, then I'll have no choice. Otherwise, you'll end up with a broken neck."

"And you'd care?"

"It's *my* neck. Or have you forgotten that you belong to me? That means when you hurt yourself, you're damaging what's *mine*." His voice rumbles on the last word, and it somehow infuses a deeper meaning into it.

Our eyes lock for a moment, then his drop to the diamonds at my throat. He touches the collar. "I don't understand."

"What?"

He peers down at the hand he's holding in his. "Long ago, there was a tribe of warriors that drank the blood of their captured enemy. They said it gave them powers over them." He lifts my hand and licks the beads of blood that have formed there.

I swallow hard, my mouth gone completely dry as I'm mesmerized by this act. The flat of his tongue is crimson as he rolls it back in and closes his eyes and tastes me. "You're inside me now." Then he looks at me with a dark hunger that stirs sensual heat in the pit of my stomach, and I believe it's true, that somehow, he's got some power over me.

"Arran," I whisper.

He presses himself between my legs and leans in, his lips so close to mine, I can almost taste them. When he exhales, I inhale, taking him in.

I move forward a centimeter, close enough for the warmth of his lips to touch mine.

"Whether you ask for it or not, I'll fuck you if you kiss me," he repeats the warning he's given me several times and will probably give several more. Because it seems that every day, I find myself in this position.

And because I'm still in denial about what I let him do to me being just as bad, just as much of a betrayal as anything else, I don't move again.

His gaze drops to my mouth at the same time as he slides his hand under my skirt. "I'll kiss you anyway," he says, low and sinfully smooth. "Here."

I shut my eyes as he shoves my panties aside and rubs the back of his knuckles softly over my slit. But I open them just as fast when he takes the backs of my legs and pushes them up, setting both of my feet on the counter. With my skirt gathered at my waist, I get a clear view of him bending over me and burying his nose in my pussy.

He breathes me in and moans as if my scent is intoxicating to him. Maybe it is. The effect he has on me is similar. A drug. A very bad, very dangerous and deadly drug.

Then he licks me once, from asshole to nub. And there he remains, concentrating his efforts on my clitoris. Sucking on it. Drawing small circles around it that way that drives me mad with need.

As I approach my climax, I hold his head to me with my bandaged hands, the pain completely forgotten. Because that's what this type of kiss is meant to do. It's meant to make me forget pain and anger and any sense of who I am.

I come, convulsing, crying out his name as I press my thighs hard around his ears. When I'm done, I fall back onto the counter, heaving. Maybe even dying a little. But I don't care.

Sweet Jesus, I'm doomed.

14

ARRAN

In the very heart of Philadelphia on a block full of shops and eateries, you'll find the upscale French bistro where famed Chef Guillaume serves his creations to very discerning patrons. He's even won a prestigious Michelin Star.

It's near impossible to get a reservation at the bistro with the gold awning that simply reads 1923. Only those with certain tastes and sizable incomes are allowed a seat. And of those, even fewer are taken through the small dining room and beyond the busy kitchen to the steel door in the back.

Innocuous though it may seem, it is a highly guarded door, for every cook in the kitchen is armed and ready. Lethal weapons to be used should anyone who's not authorized try to go beyond it.

On the other side of that steel barricade, the real security begins. A long hall with facial recognition cameras directs guests to the entrance of the most prestigious underground club in the country.

The Maxton Pierce Auction House, so named by my

father and his then partner and friend, Miles Pierce, is home to millions of dollars' worth of stolen and/or illegally acquired artifacts, jewelry, museum pieces, etc.

Skye glances at the men formally dressed in black tuxedoes as they flank us menacingly. There's a hint of resentment in her stare, possibly at being searched for weapons, but no one is above our laws here. Not even me.

"Don't you get to come in a back way?" she asks as one of the security guys runs his palms up and down her sides.

I clench my jaw as I watch him touch her, wanting to hack his limbs off. "Not when I have a guest," I say through gritted teeth.

It was a measure put in place when Miles brought in a woman who tried to kill my father. Of course, the guards were on her before she could do anything, but the fact that she'd come in through the back entrance meant she wasn't searched for a weapon. It could have ended in catastrophe.

After Skye is cleared, I press my Maxton House ring to the magnetic scanner. It reads the chip located behind the ruby and unlocks the door.

"Welcome, Arran Maxton," a computerized voice says.

"It's a key," Skye whispers, peering at the ring.

"Every member of the auction house receives one," I tell her.

The door opens and I tug her inside the darkened interior of the lavish club.

"I..." she trails off as she takes it all in. "It's huge. I didn't know it would be so big."

Of course it's big. It takes up the entire block. All of the shops on the exterior are nothing but a façade. Though few of them are operating businesses, they are all *my* businesses. Some make me money, others provide a means of escape should the need ever present itself. Alternate exits.

Skye gawks around in obvious awe, her lips slightly parted. "I'm not sure what I imagined it would be like in here, but this wasn't it." She laughs. "Though I suppose I should have expected it."

"What does that mean?" I ask.

"It reminds me of your place."

"Ah." I look around too. I've never thought about it before, but it does resemble my home, with dark tones, leather tufted chairs, and amber sconces. Even the stage at the far end of the room has deep-blue velvet curtains and an ornate mahogany wood podium and pedestal. "That would be because my father designed the place, just like he did my house."

"Oh? So it's not your taste?"

"I don't have an opinion on décor," I admit. "You don't like it?"

She sighs. "I love it, actually. It's very old world classic. It's amazing, Arran."

"You're impressed, then?" The question that comes out my mouth surprises me.

Her brows pinch slightly. "Does it matter to you that I am?"

My eyes trail her lovely features, then our gazes meet and lock. The gray of her irises darkens, smoky and seductive. Sultry.

Suddenly, I forget how to breathe. I swallow down hard as I reach to touch the collar around her throat. But before my fingertips can make contact with her skin, we're interrupted.

"Miss Cameron," Jessica, our hostess, greets. She shifts her attention to me. "Mr. Maxton."

"Michael Williams will be joining us tonight," I tell her. "Please let me know when he arrives."

Jessica glances at the tablet she's holding. "Ah, yes, he actually got here ten minutes ago and has already been escorted to your table."

"Thank you." With a palm flat against Skye's back, I guide her toward my private booth at the far end of the hall.

"Who is Michael Williams?" she asks.

"He's a client of mine. But don't worry, he's pretty anti-social and probably won't talk much. Might even choose to move once the auction starts."

Several of the staff greet us as we make our way through the tables already filling up with patrons. Dinner is served first, along with the complimentary wine to loosen those wrists for the bids.

Loud laughter roars over the chatter, calling my attention to a large table near the front. I grind my teeth as I spot Landon and his buddies hollering to each other, several empty tumblers in front of them. Fucking frat boys.

Landon notices us and lifts a glass our way, an annoying grin on his face.

"Do you think they'll make a scene?" Skye asks, grimacing as she stares at them.

"Yes," I say. "But I'll deal with it later."

Up ahead, I see the back of Michael's head as he sits at the table that's always reserved for me. A waitress is with him, showing him the list of wines he can select from.

Even from several feet away, I can't help but detect the giddiness with which she smiles as she takes the menu from him. He turns to her so that his profile comes slightly into view.

My step falters. There's something about him that suddenly strikes me as odd.

Picking up on it, Skye asks, "What's the matter?"

"I'm not sure." I approach cautiously now, my gaze narrowed on the man's dark head.

When we're about a foot away, he fully turns to me and I realize what it is that disturbed me. This isn't Michael Williams.

"Hello, Arran." He grins, a friendly smile that's completely at odds with the aura of danger that surrounds him.

As if she senses my tension, Skye stiffens. She looks between him and me.

"Who the fuck are *you*?" I angle my body so that more of me is between him and Skye.

"Have a seat and I'll tell you," he says, his mouth tugged up on one side.

"Better yet, I'll have you escorted out of my damned club and you can tell my guards who you are."

The man narrows his steel-blue eyes. "Aren't you curious as to how I made it through your secure doors and all the way to your table in the first place?" He tuts. "Your guards don't pose a threat to me. So unless you want a massacre, I suggest you sit your ass in that chair so that we can have a discussion like civilized men."

I scan the club. Not a single one on my security detail seems aware that there is an intruder. A dangerous one from what I can tell.

"You're Gideon Black," I state. There's no doubt in my mind it's him. He's the only one powerful enough to infiltrate this fortress.

He nods and extends his hand to me. For a moment, I consider leaving him hanging, but this isn't the time or the place. So I take his hand and shake it with a hard enough squeeze that were he a weak man, he'd yelp.

But Gideon Black is not a weak man. He's as powerful as

I am, and he shows it by gripping me just as tightly, all the while doing it with a grin. "Nice to finally meet you, Arran."

"How did you get in?"

"I have my ways. And just in case you're considering taking me out, know that I never do anything without an insurance policy." He glances at Skye, and her eyes goes wide. "Devon says hello, by the way."

Fuck. His insurance policy is Devon. "He's just a secretary."

"One whose life you value."

"Where is he?"

"He'll be back at the office, safe and sound, tomorrow morning."

My jaw clenches and I tear myself from his grasp. His smile broadens. The fucker has the advantage. When we break contact, he gives Skye his full attention.

His expression softens only slightly, but there's something in his eyes, like those of a wolf about to strike its prey, as he stands and greets her. "And you are?"

Her back goes ramrod straight, but she accepts his greeting. "Skye."

"Very nice to meet you, Skye." He holds on to her too long and practically leers at her, eating her up with his gaze.

"Enough!" I hiss.

Gideon gives me a knowing look before he laughs and releases her, as if I reacted exactly as he expected me to. Skye rubs her skin nervously as I glare at him.

"Why don't you two sit and have a chat with me. I promise not to take too much of your time," he says.

I weigh my options. If I call security now and Gideon truly has Devon, he could kill him. That would start a war I'd rather not initiate. Or I can listen to whatever bullshit he wants to throw my way, maybe learn something from it, and let him go, none the wiser that just a few floors below, my father sleeps. If Gideon knew, Father would already be dead. And if I seem too eager to get him out, he'll suspect.

Pulling out a chair, I motion for Skye to sit. She glances at it and the man warily but complies. Then I take the seat between them.

He sits too, that fucking smile still on his face as he watches her. "Your business is with me," I remind him. "Not my date."

"Is it?"

"It fucking better be." I place my hand over hers. "What do you want?"

He peers around the club. "Really nice place you have here, Arran. I must say, I've heard wonderful things and have been meaning to visit. I was just waiting for the invitation."

"Cut the bullshit. What do you want?"

"Wow," Gideon says with mock dismay. Then he shows me the ruby ring on his small finger. "Is this how you treat all your customers?"

I study the Maxton House ring, wondering how he got it. Is it the one that belongs to Michael Williams?

"You're not a customer," I remind him. "You're an unwelcome fly in my soup. So say what you want and get the fuck out."

Gideon's lips pull upward. His gaze moves from me to Skye, who's staring at him wide-eyed and visibly disturbed by our interaction.

Our waitress returns with the most expensive bottle of wine we offer and proceeds to pour him some. When she comes to my glass, I stop her before she's able to fill it. "When was the last time you saw me drink wine?"

The waitress seems stunned for a moment. "Whiskey. You prefer whiskey. I'll be right back with that, sir."

"That was my bad," Gideon says. "I assumed you'd have good taste."

"That's because you're an ass," I tell him.

"What about you, my dear?" he asks Skye. "What do you prefer to drink?"

She looks between us, then says, "Water."

Gideon chuckles. "Is that what you prefer, or does your master have to tell you?"

He can't see it, but I can. The tightening of her fists beneath the table and the tensing of her jaw.

I lean into her. "Why don't you go freshen up?"

"Where's the powder room?"

Pointing toward the direction of it, I say, "Take your time. I'll get rid of him before you come back."

She stares at him. "Is he dangerous?"

"Deadly," I tell her the truth.

Nodding, she stands. "Please excuse me. I need to go to the ladies' room."

I watch as she walks away a distance, stops to speak with one of the waitresses, glances back our way, then continues in the direction she's pointed toward.

"She's Thomas Cameron's daughter, isn't she?"

It doesn't surprise me that Gideon has been spying on me. And if he could get into Maxton House, he's probably already been in Asta as well. I'll have to reinforce every area of security, rescreen every staff member, and go through our software with a fine-toothed comb to make sure it hasn't been hacked.

For now, it's either make a scene that will ruin everyone's experience and have the man arrested just so he can escape anyway. Or I can have the conversation he's obviously here for and hopefully learn more about my enemy.

We peer at each other for a long while, him taking sips of my expensive wine while I drink the whiskey that was just delivered.

"So tell me. How much money does a place like this bring in?" he asks.

"I'm sure you've already investigated that yourself."

"Some."

"Are you ever going to get to the point, Gideon? What are you doing here?"

"I've gotten to the point many times, actually. Didn't you receive my letters? I want to know where Clive is." Gone is all hint of amusement. He's staring at me intensely, his nostrils flaring.

"You are out of your fucking mind if you believe I'd give him to you." I take another drink, my movements calm.

"Even when you know I have Devon?"

"No one is worth my father's life, Gideon. You're wasting your time."

Amusement lights up his features. "Are you so sure about that?"

I don't like the way he asks that, not one bit. An uneasy feeling creeps into me as I try to figure out what has him so pleased. But I shrug it off. There's no room for doubt in a conversation between enemies. "Let's say I did tell you where he is. Then what? You kill him, and let me live in peace?"

"Only if you agree to shut down all of Maxton's underground operations. You can still keep Maxton Holdings, but I want Maxton House and Asta shut down." As he says it, the lights in the hall dim by twenty five percent, letting everyone know the bidding is about to begin.

That's when I catch sight Landon at his table, making some exaggerated motion as he stands and bows to his friends.

"Why me?" I sit back in my seat. "Landon is next in line. He's right over there." I point to the table near the stage, where my brother seems to be giving a toast. "Why not harass him over this and leave me alone?"

Other than a quick glance at Landon, Gideon doesn't give him much more consideration. "He's useless. That boy probably has no idea where his own dick is, much less his father."

Of course Gideon wouldn't be fooled into believing that Landon is or will ever truly be the head of anything.

Just as the auctioneer makes his way to the podium on the stage, Landon leaves his table. I follow him across the hall with my gaze.

"You should know, I'd burn down the entire Maxton empire before I shut down Maxton House and Asta," I say to Gideon. But my eyes are still on Landon, who's now passed the bar and is heading toward the hall that leads to the bathrooms and offices.

"Because those are what have given you power," Gideon replies. "Power that Clive used to take down my father."

Landon would have no reason to go into the offices. There's nothing that's ever interested him there. The bathroom, however, has something he's definitely expressed wanting.

"Arran, you seem distracted."

I flick my gaze back to Gideon. "You know my answer. You knew it before you came, so it's beyond me why you bothered. I'll never give up my father, and I'll never give up the auction houses."

"And you know that eventually, I will find Clive. You'll be next."

Downing my whiskey in one drink, I get to my feet. "Since you've made it clear I can't take you out tonight, enjoy your stay at Maxton House. I expect Devon at work first thing tomorrow morning. If he isn't there, you will actively be sought out and killed."

He nods and relaxes back into the seat. "You'll have your man back. Don't worry."

I don't worry one bit, because right now, I have bigger problems on my hands than even this fucking sociopath the Sinacores have been searching for. I need to make sure Landon isn't near Skye.

With that on my mind, I leave behind the man who's been hunting my father for months. Let him enjoy his time in the highly secured club he's managed to infiltrate. It might be a blessing in disguise when he realizes there's nothing here for him and he leaves. But just in case...

As I make my way to the restrooms, I tug my phone from my pocket and dial Ruslan.

"Rus," he answers.

"Get your ass to Maxton House and bring some men."

"Why? What's happening?" he questions, but I can already hear him giving orders.

"Gideon Black paid me a visit. He's still here."

"The fuck? And you're letting him live?"

"He has Devon," I say.

The line goes silent as I suspected it would once I mentioned my assistant. Though neither of them have said anything to me, I know they spend a lot of time together outside of work.

Ruslan growls. "If he touches a hair on his fucking head, I'll fucking kill him myself."

"Gideon will set him free as long as we allow him to leave peacefully. But I want insurance, just in case." It irks me that I'm using the same term he did, but it's needed.

"I'll be there in less than five minutes."

"Be discreet about it," I hiss. "The last thing I want is to alert him."

"Tonight, I'll be discreet. I can't guarantee afterward. He's on my shit list now."

I hang up as the hallway comes into view, and there's no sign of Skye or Landon. Not bothering to ask the nearest security guard if he saw which way my brother went—I already know—I go to the ladies' bathroom.

But when I go in there, all I find is an angry woman staring at me through the mirror. "This is for women!"

"Is there someone else in here?" I demand.

"Just me and unfortunately you, sir."

Without bothering to apologize, I go to the men's restroom and also find it empty. My heart sinks as I look down the hall to the many doors of the administrative offices. He could have tricked her into any of them.

Furious now, I go from door to door, kicking them in with all my might, not caring that I'm calling attention to myself. I do it all for that woman with the gray eyes and the sweet pussy. The woman I consider mine, and I'm willing to leave a monster at my table to prevent her from being touched. Because she's mine, and not even Landon will ever get a taste of what she has to offer.

"Sir, is everything all right?" Two of my guards appear. They glance at each other, unsure what to do.

"Find my fucking brother!" I order and turn to the small crowd that has begun to gather at the far end of the hall.

Fuck priorities and making scenes, and fuck Gideon Black. All I want is Skye.

15

SKYE

Every step I take toward the ladies' room is an agonizing testament to the fact that I'm in so much shock, I can't properly react. If I could, I'd be shaking so badly, walking would be impossible.

Gideon Black is here. He somehow managed to break through the fortress that is Maxton House and sit at Arran's table, looking happy as a clam. Like the cocky billionaire who belongs there.

Was it a show of power for Arran's benefit or mine? Did he come to threaten him somehow, or to remind me that I still have a task and his patience is wearing thin?

"I never do anything without an insurance policy."

He was talking about Maisie, I'm sure of it.

It doesn't matter. The fact that he was able to come here without a problem tells me how resourceful he is. If I don't manage to get what he wants from me, there's no place far enough to hide.

I enter the bathroom and go straight for the sink, turn on the faucet, and splash water on my face. So what that my makeup might get messy? I'm too flustered to care.

God, the way Gideon watched me with amusement sent a shiver down my spine I still can't dispel. Like I was a little bug he was playing with and could squash at any moment. A single word from him to let Arran know that I'm his spy, and it would have been over for me. He wouldn't have to lift a finger. Arran would kill me himself.

Or would he?

My hand begins to shake as I peer at it. It's the one he engulfed with his large one, as if he sensed my distress at the table. Just moments earlier, he'd placed his body defensively between Gideon and me.

If he were to find out about my arrangement with his enemy, would he throw me out? Or would he still see me as *his*. Something to guard and protect. It is possible he views me as his enemy now yet still shielded me?

A glint of light in my reflection catches my attention. It's the collar, twinkling prettily. A cold reminder that regardless of how possessive Arran might be when it comes to me, I'll never be anything more than an actual possession to him. And possessions are easily discarded.

Tearing a paper towel out of the holder, I dab water droplets off my face and smooth the waves in my hair.

A woman enters the restroom, and immediately, her eyes meet mine in the mirror. By the way she's dressed, I assume she's one of the hostesses. "Is your name Skye Cameron?"

"Yes."

"Mr. Maxton asked me to come check on you. Is everything all right?"

My brows pinch together. "It is. He's the one who sent me here. He needed a minute alone with a client."

Now it's her turn to frown. "Uh. Well, he's asked that I

show you to the admin office when you're finished. He's waiting there for you."

I smile at her. "I'm done now."

After one last glimpse at myself, I follow her out. She makes a left, moving away from the auction, which, from the sound of it, is now in full swing.

"Sixth Dynasty, Egyptian gold falcon vessel, listed as number four hundred ten in the catalogue. Item is considered lost, and listing rules must be followed," the auctioneer calls loudly. "Bidding starts at one hundred thousand..."

"The last door to the right," the woman indicates, stopping midway.

"Thank you." I continue on down the hall to the room Arran is waiting for me in. I knock and listen for the muffled order to enter before doing so. "The amount of money in this place is ins—"

A hand clamps over my mouth the moment I step foot inside. The door is slammed shut behind me, and then I'm being unceremoniously pushed farther in until my ass hits a desk.

"Hello, beautiful."

My eyes widen in horror as I realize it's not Arran who was waiting for me at all. But Landon.

He smiles and his handsome features distort, like the Joker effect someone achieves from putting a flashlight under their face. I've never been fond of clowns, and this takes it to a whole new level of terrifying.

I slam my palms against his chest and push with all my might. But just like at Arran's house, Landon is a brick wall. Instead of budging an inch, he shoves harder into me, his hand digging into my face, threatening to cover my nose too.

"Shh. Calm down," he coos. "I just want to talk."

Glaring at him, I stop fighting. He eases his hand from my mouth, his grin broadening. "Good girl." Then he trails his fingers over my cheek and tucks some of my hair behind my ear. "How is it that my brother always gets the rare finds?"

"Maybe he's just lucky," I say.

"Sometimes we have to make our own luck." He traces my jawbone, moving to my chin. With his thumb, he touches my lower lip, his gaze on it as if he can imagine dipping into my mouth the way Arran did.

"I'll bite it off," I whisper, completely disgusted by the thought of any part of him inside any part of me.

Smirking, he says, "I might just like that."

Before I can react, my hair is in his fist, holding my head firmly as he kisses me. Revulsion hits me full blast and I heave at the same time as I clinch my teeth to prevent his tongue from delving in.

I push as he tugs, his free hand tearing at the décolletage of my dress. He presses into me so hard, my butt is forced onto the desk and my legs spread. I gasp as he yanks my head back to lick my neck.

His bulge rubs over my core and he moans. "You're going to be so tight, aren't you, Skye? I can tell. So fucking tight."

He continues on, but I tune him out. Instead, I focus on a solution to my predicament. Landon is much bigger and stronger than I am. Which means I will need lots of momentum.

I slap my hands behind me, hoping that like any other desk, it will have sharp, heavy objects. It does.

Although I have no clue what it is, my fingers wrap around the thing, and without waiting another second, I swing it forward with all my might. There's a crack as it meets Landon's jaw. However, to my misfortune, it only stuns him momentarily.

Angry now, he comes at me again. But before he can get to me, I roll out of reach, tripping on my own feet as I attempt to get away.

The instant I land on the floor, I twist and fling my arms out defensively. But I don't need to worry about him anymore.

Now it's he who's pinned to the desk. He who's fighting against someone much stronger.

I didn't even hear Arran come in. Yet there he is, an avenging demon, furious and beautifully terrifying. With a single hand to Landon's throat, he's holding him in place, seated on the desk the same way I was.

Landon struggles to free himself, but all he manages to do is turn a bright shade of red.

"You fucking touched her," Arran growls, low and so menacing that even I feel the need to recoil.

I scramble to my feet and plaster myself against the wall. But I don't leave. I can't. Instead, I remain there, watching Arran in complete fascination.

"She's just a fucking whore," Landon manages to screech. "I'll pay you if that's what you're worried about. I have the money."

Arran turns his head slightly, as if he's searching for me. When his eyes meet mine, he says, "No one touches her."

What happens next is all a blur of motion. There's a glint of metal as it slices through the air and downward. A loud thud is followed by a short, shrill sound as Landon sucks in a breath. His mouth remains open on a mute scream, his eyeballs bulging from their sockets.

I want to scream too when I finally register what's

happened, but like Landon, my voice remains lodged in my throat at the horror of it.

Arran twists the knife he's just jammed into the desk, right between Landon's legs. And from the amount of blood oozing through his black slacks and dripping onto the floor, I'd say something was slashed in the process.

After what seems like an eternity, Landon finally breathes. But he doesn't move, and my bet is that he's afraid to lose more than he already has.

He shuts his eyes tightly and gasps. "I'll fu— I'll fucking kill you."

"I bet you won't have the balls to do it." Arran laughs, infusing sarcasm into it. "You're lucky I don't do what I really want to and gut you."

Twisting the blade, he leans in closer. Landon begins to tremble uncontrollably, whether from fear or shock, I'm not sure. "Don't move or you'll lose more than your nuts. Though I can't really be sure that's all I snipped. Doubt anyone will miss your dick if I got it too."

"Fuck you and your whore!" Spittle dribbles from his lips.

"Shit!" A large tattooed guy curses as he rushes in but stops dead in his tracks when he takes in the scene. He throws an arm over his eyes like he can't bear the sight of it, and I don't blame him. "Fuck!"

Though I'm sure he hears him, Arran doesn't look behind him. Instead, he says to Landon, "Stay put or the damage will be worse." He takes a step back. "Stay," he repeats, lifting a finger to him as if he were a dog. "Ruslan here is going to help you."

"The fuck I am. You chopped off his dick!" the large man complains.

Arran ignores him. "Once you're all patched up, I want you to go back to Mother and stay there. If I ever see you again, if you ever so much as breathe near Skye, I will kill you. Do you understand?"

Landon gives him a short nod, then averts his gaze.

Arran turns to me now. His stare bores into mine as his jaw clenches and unclenches.

"Rus," he says without taking his eyes off me. "Take care of this piece of shit."

Ruslan shakes his head. "You're going to owe me big for this one."

"Just do it!" Arran hisses. Then he comes to me and snatches my wrist. Without another word, he tugs me out of the room and through the door across the hall that's now filled with security.

We're in a nondescript office like the one we just came from. He moves us behind the desk to another door that I assume is a closet with a lock.

Arran presses in a code and the electronic mechanism unlocks. To my surprise, beyond the door is another hall, this one narrow and long. At the end is a very modern high-tech steel elevator, complete with several cameras and a touch screen. He places his palm on it, and the elevator doors slide open.

We step inside, and this time, Arran has to put his face close to a retinal scanner. The elevator descends for what seems like forever, especially in the heavy silence, where all I can hear is the grinding of his teeth. The entire way, he keeps his hold on my wrist, tight and secure. I only attempt to tug at it once, and that's all I need to do to know he's not planning on letting go, his grip intensifying.

"Where are we going?" I ask when the doors open and

we exit onto a floor that could belong in any swanky office building, only, without windows.

"My office."

16

SKYE

I peek into every room we pass as we move down a wide hall with abstract artwork hung on sleek wood-paneled walls. While there are some armed men, obviously guards, milling about, it's not near as busy as it was on the upper level.

A few yards away, an older woman steps out of a room, holding a silver tray laden with prescription bottles and what looks to be the remnants of a meal.

"Arran!" She looks up in surprise, glances between us, then quickly ducks back inside. Before I can question Arran anymore on where we are and who that was, he pulls me around a corner and into one of the rooms.

Jaw working furiously, he kicks the door shut and, finally, he releases me. He stalks over to a massive glass-top desk and back to me.

Breathing raggedly, he pauses and lifts his blue stare to me. "Did he manage to...?"

I shake my head. "There might be some bruises, but that's all."

Then he's on me. His fingers are on my throat, thumbs

stroking the thin collar. Then his eyes are following the movement of his hands as he inspects me, turning my face from side to side, as if he needs to see for himself that I'm untouched.

"He didn't," I reassure him. "You got there in time."

Suddenly, he's shaking. He digs his fingers through my hair and drops his forehead to mine. Pressing his entire body against me, he breathes me in. "I should have killed him. He should be dead."

"No. Arran, he's your brother."

"And that's all that kept him alive."

Against my better judgement, I snake my arms around him, placing my palms flat against his muscled back. Because I'm trembling too. And I also need the reassurance that I'm all right. That I'm safe.

I close my lids and inhale, sucking in his now familiar male scent, taking in his heat. "Arran." His name comes out like a plea, though I'm unsure of what I'm asking for.

He goes rigid, his fingers like steel in my hair. A long moment passes between us, the tension building even though we're not looking at each other.

Then he pulls away, and his gaze drops to the damned choker and stays there. When he reaches for it and says, "Ask me to fuck you, Skye." I slap his hand away.

"No," I practically snarl, anger rising in my chest. Suddenly, I can't stand him. Can't stand the nearness of him and what it does to me.

Out of sheer frustration that he should have any effect on me, that I should feel liquid heat build in my belly at the mere idea of belonging to him, I slap his cheek.

Blue fire sparks to life in his stare and it consumes me. I try to hit him again, but he snatches my wrist an inch from his face.

Turning it, he bites the tender flesh until I wince. And, still, his eyes burn me and make me ache for him.

"Tell me to fuck you, Skye," he repeats, this time through gritted teeth.

"If you want it so bad, take it. Take what you want. Nothing's in your way. I belong to you, remember?"

"Tell me."

"Oh my God, you want my consent. Is that it?" I laugh. "Why do you need my consent now? None of this is my consent. No one asked me if I wanted my father to die, or if I wanted to sell myself like a thing just to keep my sister a—"

Arran's eyes narrow as he processes what I've said. What I was about to say. And I realize that if I don't act now, I may have just given away too much.

Before he can utter a single word, I pounce. My arms go around his neck and I press my lips to his. If I ever doubted what he said about a kiss being the point of no return, his immediate and combustive response to it is all the confirmation I need.

I understand him now, because, damn me, I can't help but respond to it too. It's a primal physical reaction, an explosion of need and desire deep inside me that's brought on by the feel of his tongue sliding across mine. The taste of him in my mouth. His breath blowing into my lungs every time he exhales.

His kiss overrides any sense of self, of dignity and pride. I no longer care that he owns me or that I've been robbed of choices. All that matters in this moment is the hunger to be possessed by him. I want to be his, and if I was given the choice, right here, right now, I'd still be his.

With his hands on my ass, Arran lifts me. I wrap my legs around his waist as he walks us to the wall, slamming me into it. He deepens the kiss as he grinds into me, and I moan from the pleasure of the friction against my sex.

He slides his hand between us, and I'm so acutely aware of every touch, I cry out without breaking away from his lips.

After releasing himself from his pants, he pushes aside the scrap of fabric covering my pussy and thrusts. This time, I do break the kiss. I gasp at the intrusion of his cock inside me, stretching me, ramming into me painfully, achingly hard.

But he doesn't give me time to catch my breath. I don't think he can, and I don't want him to. I like this too much.

He drops his face into the crook of my neck as he hammers into me. Distantly, I register the sound of fabric tearing, a frame falling and glass breaking. I'm mindless, unable to do anything but hold on to him and let the beast in him find its release.

When it does, it's with a guttural growl. He tenses, his thrusts slowing but each more powerful than the last. I can feel his cock pulsating as he pumps himself into me, filling me with his cum, just like he promised.

As his orgasm ebbs, he pulls back slightly and peers into my face. The strain he showed just a few minutes ago is now gone.

He cups my cheek as something strange passes over his expression. When he leans in to kiss me again, I expect the same raw passion, but all he does is graze my lips achingly sweet. Quick and barely there, but I feel it all the way to the marrow of my bones.

His lips part as if he's about to say something important, something that could change the dynamic of our relationship. But he doesn't get a chance, because a knock at the door interrupts us.

"Arran, you in there?"

Arran's mouth tugs into a straight line. "It's Ruslan." He pulls out of me, and warm liquid trickles from my sex and down my thigh. "Give me a moment," he yells to the man.

From a cabinet, he produces a roll of paper towels. Tearing one off, he hands it to me.

I wipe quickly and adjust my dress. When I'm somewhat decent, I nod to him and he opens the door.

Ruslan enters, giving me a side-glance as he does. Probably because he can tell what we were doing in here.

"Landon's at the hospital," he says to Arran. "Soon as he's stitched up, he'll be on his way to Mommy's house."

"All done discreetly, I assume."

"Very. But it's costing you a lot of money to keep people from talking."

Arran gives him a look. "I don't care. Pay whatever it takes." He goes to a panel on the wall and pushes it in. It spins, revealing a lazy Susan type of shelf with many types of liquor. "What about Gideon?"

My ears perk up, but when Arran's brow furrows as he watches me, I feign interest in my shoes.

"There was no trace of him. By the time I got here, he was gone. I was actually searching for you to ask if you knew where he went. He also let Devon go. I just got a call from him telling me he's back home with no memory of what happened."

"Gideon knocked him out."

Ruslan nods. "Probably for the best."

"I want you to go through all the security footage. Figure out how that fuck got in so easily. And get a call in to Michael Williams. Make sure Gideon didn't kill him to get his ring."

"Yes, sir," Ruslan says. "Will you be staying here?"

Arran gives me a suspicious glance. "I'm going home. You and I will reconvene tomorrow."

———

I'm left alone in Arran's office while he goes to do things he obviously doesn't want me around for.

I scan the room. It's not cluttered, not that I expected it to be, but there are more hints that this place is used on a daily basis. Unlike his office at home, his desk here has random items, like a notepad with actual notes in it scribbled in Arran's neat but stern writing, a few files stacked in the corner, and a cup with pens. On one side of the room is a coatrack, and on the other, three file cabinets.

Digging through a single one of these drawers would probably prove much more fruitful than anything I've done at his house. The temptation to go through everything is great. But I have no idea how long he'll be gone.

So I sit at the chair behind his desk and lean back to stare at the ceiling, though I'm not looking at it, not really. What I see instead is the expression on Arran's face just before we were interrupted by Ruslan. I wonder what he was about to say? Does it matter?

They say actions speak louder than words. Had Arran already said what he wanted to when he attacked his own brother in my defense? Yes, I'm his to protect, but to have done what he did, I've got to be more than just an object to him.

Then again, I can also recall with vivid clarity each and every time he's touched my collar and the sting of knowing he views me as a thing. No, not just a thing. An object of revenge.

"Skye. It's time to go." Arran comes in with a long black coat. When I stand, he holds it out for me.

"Thanks, but I wasn't chilly."

"Your dress is torn."

I frown as, for the first time, I notice the torn décolletage and how the slit of the skirt that came to my thigh is now up to my waist. With everything that happened, I never looked at myself.

"I didn't realize how badly Landon tore it," I say, futilely attempting to hold the pieces together. No wonder Ruslan barely glanced my way.

"It wasn't Landon." Arran's gaze intensifies, giving meaning to his words. *It was me.*

"Oh," I say. "Well, it's just a dress."

He lowers his eyes. "We should go." Then he takes my hand and leads me out.

Five minutes later, we're out the door and sliding into the back seat of Arran's black car.

"Take us home, Frank," he tells his driver.

"Sure thing, boss."

I stare out the window the entire drive, and as the city goes by in a blur of lights, the adrenaline that was keeping me going begins to wear off.

By the time Frank pulls up to the entrance of the house on Rittenhouse Square, my limbs feel like they've been pumped full of lead, heavy and hard to move.

"Can we just sleep in the car?" I lay my head back and blow out a long held breath.

"It's tempting, but no."

Frank comes around to the door and opens it. Arran steps out, then extends his hand to me. I take it and allow him to pull me out into the cool night air.

"I'll see you tomorrow, sir," Frank says as he goes to get back into the vehicle.

"Have a good night."

We start to make our way to the front door, but Arran stops, his brows pinched together tightly as he stares ahead, then all around us.

My heart leaps into my chest at his expression. "What is it?"

"Something's wrong." He tugs me a step back. "The lights—"

He throws himself on me just as a loud boom erupts. A hot blast of air hits us like a sledgehammer and we both go down hard, my head bouncing off the sidewalk with a nasty crack. Sharp pain spreads through my skull like a wildfire, and I scream.

Then everything goes black.

17

SKYE

"Skye! Skye!" I hear someone calling to me in the distance.

I open my eyes and realize it's not distant at all, but right before me. The blurry image of a man hovering over me begins to clear, but his voice is still muted and hollow-sounding. Behind him, huge orange flames lick the dark sky, weaving in and out of rolling clouds of smoke.

"Arran?"

"Can you stand?" he asks, concern written all over his face.

I shake my head, trying to clear it. I can hear better, but I'm still a bit dizzy.

"Shit." He lifts me, and then he's running with me in his arms toward a vehicle coming at us in reverse.

It screeches to a halt in front of us. Arran opens the door and shoves me inside before he gets in too.

"Go, go, go!" Arran yells.

I'm pressed into the seat as Frank floors it, and it takes me a few tries to right myself and strap in. He makes so many turns that I eventually lose track of where we are. That is, until we get on I-76 and Frank merges into traffic.

"Are we being followed?" he asks, peering through the rearview mirror.

Arran looks out the back window. "No." Then he turns to me, and in much the same way he examined me at the auction house, his hands are everywhere, searching. "What hurts?"

I touch the spot at the back of my head and wince. "I think it's just a bruise. What happened?"

"Someone bombed my house."

He says it so matter-of-factly that it takes me a moment to ask, "Who?"

"I don't know, but I can guess." Arran tugs out his phone and dials someone.

"The man at the table," I say. "Gideon Black?"

He nods. "Fuck! Charles isn't answering."

Even though they don't believe we're being followed, I can't help the occasional glance through every window, just to make sure. Arran is doing the same thing.

"How did you know?" I ask. "You figured something was wrong."

He dials another number and presses the phone to his ear. As it rings, he says to me, "All the lights were out in the house and the guard's station across the street."

My brow furrows. "What guard station?"

"I own the building across the street," he clarifies. "The second floor has a direct view of the house. I have ten men stationed there. The lights were off there too."

"Oh." I'd wondered how he could have so much security at his places of business, yet only three men to guard his home.

"Where do you want me to take you?" Frank asks. "Maxton House?"

"Negative," Arran replies, hanging up and dialing another number.

"Why not?" I question. "Didn't you say it was the most secure place you have?"

"We can't go back there."

"But we could rest there and—"

"I said no!" he cuts me off.

My mouth slams shut and it's all I can do not to growl at him. "What about my house? No one would think to look for you there."

Arran smirks. "But *everyone* would think to look for *you* there."

"What about your father's place?" Frank suggests. "It's still secured."

He remains quiet for a long moment. Then his breathing pattern changes, probably not noticeably enough to anyone else, anyone who isn't always paying attention to his every move the way I do. But I catch that hitch in his throat, as if he's forcing air through a suddenly tight space.

"I can't go there," he finally says.

"Your mother?"

"She lives in Paris. Besides, with Landon being her favorite, I doubt she'd feel hospitable toward me right now."

I sigh and sink into the seat, hugging myself. "There must be somewhere. We can't drive around all night."

"I know a place." Arran pinches the bridge of his nose. "Frank, take us to Briar House."

I drift in and out of sleep during the entire hour-and-a-half drive to Todt Hill, a beautiful neighborhood on Staten Island. After offering multiple options of places we could go to, Arran told me about Briar House, the old Victorian mansion we're headed to, and the most secure location he could think of. It belongs to the king of the New York underworld, Luca Sinacore.

At first, every time I drift off, I'm assaulted by the feeling of freefalling, helpless and powerless, jumping every few minutes. Arran just stares at me like I'm crazy. But after a while, he moves closer and wraps an arm around me, bringing me into him tightly. Like a swaddled baby, once I'm secured, I sleep deeply and soundly.

The car coming to a stop wakes me, that dreaded feeling of falling returning full force.

Arran's arm tightens around me to keep me still. "We're here."

"What time is it?" It's still dark outside, the bright lights of the portico we've parked under making everything else seem ominously black.

"One thirty."

The door is opened for us and Arran steps out, then extends his hand to help me. We're greeted by several armed men, all wearing earpieces and matching severe expressions that warn of their deadliness.

From the entrance, a man with shoulder-length hair, who's maybe somewhere in his mid-thirties, comes out wearing black jeans, a white T-shirt, and unlaced black combat boots. Behind him, a woman appears. She's also in a somewhat disheveled state, wearing gray sweats and a hoodie, her hair mussed like she just woke up.

"Luca." Arran shakes the man's hand. "I apologize for crashing in like this in the middle of the night."

"Thank her." Luca points his thumb over his shoulder toward the woman. "She's the one who took the call."

"Thank you, Carina."

She moves forward and hugs him. Arran stiffens but doesn't push her away. "I'm glad you guys are all right." Looking at me, she asks, "And you are?"

"Skye," I reply. "I'm Arran's..." I trail off, unsure how to finish that.

As if she can sense my discomfort, she gives me a hug too. "Welcome, Skye. I'm Carina, Luca's wife."

"Nice to meet you."

She pulls away and gives me a warm smile. "Why don't we get inside? I'm sure you guys are exhausted after everything that's happened." Then to Arran, she says, "You can have your driver park in the garage. One of the guys can get him set up if he wants to stay."

We follow the couple into the house. It's quiet, most of the rooms dark except for the grand foyer we step into.

"Are either of you hungry?" Carina asks. Both Arran and I shake our heads. "Okay, then, why don't I show you to your room. I know there's a lot that needs to be discussed, but it's late, and it will be better for everyone if we hold off until the morning when our brains are fully functioning."

"It will also give me time to call in Noah, Gavin, and Rowan," Luca says.

Arran scowls. "I don't believe it will be necessary to involve them. We just need a place for the night."

"Your house was just fucking blown up. Clearly you need more than that."

Arran grinds his jaw. "It's no one's concern but my own."

Taking a step toward him, Luca lowers his tone as he says, "If it has to do with Black, it's all of our concern."

Carina sighs and stands between them. "This is exactly what I mean. Luca, go back to bed. You're still drunk. I'll handle this."

He gives her a look that promises retribution but doesn't argue. Instead, he spins on his heel and goes up the staircase. In the distance, a door slams.

"Sorry about that," she says, mostly to me. "His friend, Gunn, came over last night and they had one too many. Shall we?"

She continues up the stairs, making a right at the top and then going down a long hall. We enter a lovely suite with Louis the XVI style furniture, the wood painted a light sage green with delicate garlands carved around the borders. An airy white comforter and fluffy pillows add an inviting touch that has me gravitating toward the bed, desperate to lie in it and close my eyes.

"You guys can stay here as long as you'd like," Carina says.

"We'll just need tonight," Arran insists.

Her lips pull into a straight line, and with her hands on her hips, she says, "You are just so difficult, Arran. I don't understand it. Out of all the men, you have the most to lose."

"You'll say anything to get me to join your alliance."

I glance between the two. "Alliance?"

Carina sighs. "We'll talk about it tomorrow. For now—" She pauses mid-sentence as her gaze catches on my body.

Peering down at myself, I realize the long coat has come open, exposing the beautiful but torn gown. Closing it quickly, I say, "It's been a long day."

"So it would seem. Hang on." She disappears for a few minutes, and when she returns, she has a bundle of clothes in her arms. Setting them on the bed, she splits them into two piles. "This is for you. And this is for Arran. They're just shirts, leggings, and sweatpants. We can get more clothes later."

"Thanks," I say, truly grateful.

"There are toiletries in the cabinet." She points to the en suite bathroom. "Toothbrushes, paste, hair products, stuff like that."

"We're good for now, Carina. Thank you," Arran says.

"I'll see you two downstairs in the morning." Throwing Arran a little satisfied smirk, she leaves us, shutting the door quietly behind her.

Taking off my shoes, I move farther into the room, exploring. "It was really nice of them to let us stay here."

Arran huffs as he sits at the edge of the bed and tugs off his tie. "It's not what I would have preferred. But for now, there isn't a choice. In the morning I'll leave to handle the mess."

"Is Luca your enemy?" I peek into the bathroom, my eyes focusing on the claw-foot tub that's just calling to me.

"Well, he's not exactly a friend."

I begin to undress, tossing the coat onto a nearby chair and the gown in the trash bin. "Carina seemed friendly."

"That's because she wants something from me. It's called cunning."

"The alliance?" I ask, recalling the word he used.

He nods. "Gideon Black's father was killed years ago by a group of men. Now he's out for revenge, and some of the families in power have come together to fight him."

"Is he after you?" Though I know the answer—I can put two and two together—I want confirmation. Was Clive one of the men who killed Gideon's father?

"He's after my father," Arran replies.

"Why don't you join the alliance, then? It would make sense."

"I don't want anyone telling me what to do. Especially not those two." He points in the direction of where Luca and Carina's room is.

"If you dislike them so much, why did we come here? Frank said your father's house is also secure."

His eyes narrow as he stares at me, and I can see the battle inside him. Like the reason he'd rather be here than in his own family home is significant, and he wants to tell me. But it would let me in and I'd see whatever he wants to keep hidden.

Instead, he asks, "How's your head?"

I touch the spot that made contact with the pavement. "A bit sore but much better."

He stands and takes off his clothes, effectively distracting me from whatever it was that I'd asked before. "We're filthy. Let's take a shower."

Walking past me, he goes into the bathroom, straight for the tub. He slides the white curtain over and turns on the jets. In no time, steam is swirling through the room.

"Come," he says, motioning me over. I get in, and he steps in behind me. Tenderly, he washes my hair.

"You can scrub harder," I tell him. "It doesn't really hurt anymore."

"First thing tomorrow, I'm calling the doctor. I want you checked out."

"Do I have a say?"

"No."

Rolling my eyes, I sigh but don't argue. Especially not when the way he washes me is a balm, soothing away the troubles of the day. His fingers dig just deep enough into the sore muscles of my shoulders and back.

When his large hands come around and cup my breasts, I let my head drop against his chest. God, it feels so good to be bathed by him. Calming and arousing at the same time.

It must be the same for him, because his cock slowly makes its presence known, poking big and hard between my legs.

But he doesn't make an effort to penetrate. Simply keeps on rubbing me, putting me in a hypnotic spell. Getting me wetter by the second as his fingers kneed and pinch my nipples, but I'm so sleepy, all I can do is enjoy the ride.

He drops a hand to clean between my legs, his deft fingers sliding into the folds of my pussy as the head of his cock gently strokes over the entrance.

All too soon, the shower is over, and he's helping me out of the tub. After drying me with a fluffy towel, he wraps it over my shoulders and guides me to the bed.

"Lie down," he instructs.

"Aren't you tired?" I ask.

"Yes, but I want to come. And I told you that once I fucked you, there would only be one place I'd ever do that again."

"In my pussy," I whisper breathily. God, why does the thought of him filling me heat me up like this?

He tugs on the towel and it drops to the floor. "Get on the bed," he repeats.

I do as he says, lying on my back. He climbs onto the mattress, positioning himself on his knees, towering over me, his gaze roving my body.

"Spread your legs for me, Skye."

Again, I do as he says. He leans forward, sliding his palms from my clavicle to my breasts. I mewl when he bends down and takes each of my nipples into his mouth, sucking on them, grazing them with his teeth.

Then he sits back as he grips his shaft in his hand and places it against my entrance. He pushes and I inhale as he slides in all the way to the hilt. When he pulses inside me, I release my breath and suck in another as he slowly pulls out.

I'm not sure what's more intense, a hard fuck or this drawn-out torture where I can feel every inch of him moving in and out, his balls against my asshole or just the tip of his dick at my entrance. Everything is more pronounced, more obvious somehow.

And all the while, his eyes remain locked on the place where we're joined, an expression of reverence on his face.

"My cock belongs in your pussy, Skye." He slides in, out. In, out. "Do you believe that?"

I bite my lower lip and moan. "Yes."

His eyes flick up and penetrate mine. Then his hand wraps around my neck, around that thing he's placed there that marks me as his, and he says gruffly, his thrusts increasing in tempo, "It's *me* who belongs inside you."

"Yes." I sigh, though I sense there's something more to that statement. Or maybe it's not a statement at all but a question.

Now he's pounding, his grip tight on my throat, not to strangle me, but to hold his control over me. A hold he loses when I wrap my arms and legs around him and bring him down to me for the kiss I need to find my release.

I slip my tongue into his mouth, filling mine with the taste of him. My climax hits blindingly hard. I bite his lips and pump my hips upward, desperate for more friction on my clit as I ride the wave, my fingernails digging into the skin of his ass.

Arran growls but doesn't stop me from hurting him. In fact, I think he revels in the pain, because it pushes him toward his own orgasm.

When he's done, he lifts himself from me. I let him go easily, my limbs like noodles.

He's scowling, but I don't care. I'm too high.

"That was amazing," I say, my tone lazy. "Are you mad I didn't let you choke me?"

His brows pinch. "That's not what I was doing. And no, I'm not mad."

I swipe a lock of golden hair from his forehead. "I like you coming inside me. What does that make me? A whore?"

Down low, his dick twitches, and he smiles. "It makes you mine."

He bends to kiss my neck before he rolls off, dropping onto his back, his eyes closed.

Propping myself on my elbow, I peer down at him. Damn, he's hot as hell.

"Why are you scowling at me?" he asks.

I purse my lips. "How did you know?"

"I can feel it."

Exasperatedly, I say, "I wish I found you gross."

"Wow. I'm not really sure what that means, but—"

"You're too sexy to be the villain in this story, Arran. Why can't you be one of the good guys?"

"You wouldn't want me if I was."

"That's a load of shit."

"Is it?" Before I can react, he's flipped me over onto my belly. One hand is pressed into the pillow beside my head, while the other is pinning my wrist to my lower back.

He slides his cock, big and erect even this soon, over the crack of my ass and the slit of my pussy. Then he bites down on the crook of my neck, hard enough to make me cry out. But instead of shoving him off, I lift my butt, grinding myself into him.

Moving his warm lips to my ear, he says roughly, "If I was a good guy, I'd be too afraid to hurt you a little." He tightens the grip on my wrist as he places the tip of his cock at my entrance. "And you like it when I do."

I gasp as he thrusts into my still-wet pussy. But even though I've been primed, it's a shock to have him inside like that. He fucks me like a madman this time, nothing slow about it. It's rough as he takes his pleasure. And yes, it fucking turns me on.

But just as he hurts me, I do the same to him, clawing my nails into the skin of his thighs, digging them deep, urging him to also go deeper. Harder.

"Fuck me, Arran. Don't stop. Don't fucking stop."

He growls, grazing my shoulders, neck, anything he can get to with his teeth. When he's near the edge, he releases my wrist and digs between my legs. His fingers find my clit and tease it, forcing me to the point of climax just before he reaches his.

Falling limply onto me, he takes a moment to catch his breath. Then he does something so unexpected, it confuses me more about everything that has to do with him. He kisses away the sting of his bites.

I don't move for a while after he rolls off. Just lie there with my face in the pillow. When I do finally move, I find him staring at the ceiling, stiffer than I've ever seen him.

"What is it?" I turn my head to look at it too, noticing for the first time the mural done in very muted colors. Pink cherubs hold golden harps and violins, looking back at us from a light-blue sky. "It's pretty."

"There's one very similar in Kate's room in my father's home."

My lips part as I realize why he didn't want to go there. "She was killed there before she was taken to the Vellermo Art Institute, wasn't she?"

"In the kitchen." He swallows hard, then shuts his eyes as if he can't bear to view the mural any longer. "I haven't been back since her funeral."

A great big lump forms in my throat as I imagine what it would be like to lose my little sister that way. So brutally and in our own home. I'd never be able to return either.

"I'm so sorry," I whisper, reaching for him, wanting to impart some sort of comfort.

But he yanks his arm out of my grasp and sits up abruptly with his back to me. "Sorry doesn't bring her back. Nothing can bring her back."

Not even Thomas's death. He doesn't say it, but I can almost hear the angry thoughts.

Sitting up too, I hug my knees to my chest. "I know you want it to be my father. You need someone to blame." I sigh. "He did questionable things, Arran. Bad things he believed were for the greater good. But I know the man who raised me with so much love and taught me to fight for justice would never have hurt someone innocent."

"He did it, Skye. He put the hit on her."

"No, he didn't."

Turning to me, he simply smiles and touches my cheek. "You're not going to waver, are you? I've protected you, I've been inside you, and, still, you defend him."

"I've known you for a little over a week, Arran. Just because I like your big dick, doesn't suddenly erase my love and loyalty to my father."

I can't tell if he's still angry or if he wants to laugh. "Loyalty in the face of the enemy is brave. You're a very brave girl, Skye."

"So you're still my enemy?"

He leans in and kisses me. "You have your beliefs, I have mine. As long as you're Thomas's daughter, you are the enemy."

"Maybe I'll prove you wrong one day, Arran."

"I'm never wrong."

I roll my eyes at him, then grin. "Being your enemy isn't so bad."

"Because of my big dick?" Now he does laugh.

Shoving him, I allow myself to laugh too. I don't know when I'll have another chance. But the moment passes quickly because there's no real happiness in it. Just a thing that struck us both as funny.

"I was close to my dad," I tell him, sharing something I'm not sure he cares to hear. But I want to know more. "Are you close to yours?"

He remains quiet for a long while. "I used to be. Now it seems all I do is everything he doesn't want me to. Even when it's for his own good."

"What do you mean?" I ask the question, not expecting an answer at all.

"With Gideon after him, I've had to take measures to hide him. He doesn't like it." He lets out a long breath. "He's done bad things, just like your father. But I'm going to protect him anyway."

"Only, I didn't get to protect mine, did I?" I sigh in defeat. In utter disappointment. "I didn't even get to mourn him. He was killed and left splayed out in the men's bathroom to add insult to injury. Whoever did it wanted him humiliated. And while they plastered the picture all over the evening news..." as I say that, something begins to niggle at the back of my mind. "I ran."

"You did what you had to do."

I nod, but not to what he's saying. My mind is going back, to another time where I thought something very similar. About a brutal murder and a body left on display for humiliation.

Kate Maxton.

18

ARRAN

I trace the curve of Skye's spine with my fingertips. She hugs the pillow tighter beneath her head and mewls.

"Skye," I say. "It's time to get up."

Her lids flutter open and she turns sleepy gray eyes to me. A soft smile touches her lips. "You're wearing the same suit?"

"Slipping into Luca's pants doesn't sit well with me."

Wiping a palm over her face, she yawns. "I'm so tired."

"You can sleep more in the car. Right now, I'm anxious to plan my next move."

A crease forms between her brows. "Will you have to deal with Landon too?"

"No," I say, sliding my hand over her hip, unable to keep myself from touching her. "He underwent surgery last night and should be on his way to Paris by the end of the day."

"So he's fine?"

"All he lost was a nut. He'll be fine. Especially after Mother babies him the way she usually does. She might even buy him a bigger set of balls."

She laughs, then covers her mouth. "Sorry. It's not funny."

I smile in return. "It kind of is."

As if she can't help herself either, she reaches for me, grasping my wrist gently. Grinning slyly, she asks, "Does your mother baby you too?"

"I'm not so sure she's ever seen me as her child, much less a baby."

Her smile fades and there's something in her eyes, that haunting shadow that makes her seem so vulnerable. I stay like that for a moment, unable to move, captivated by her. But I know, if I remain too long in that vulnerability, she'll gain more power over me than she already has.

So I lean in and kiss her, forcing her to shut her eyes and release me.

But when I attempt to pull away, she grips me tighter and keeps me by her side. "Arran." She swallows hard. "What you did... You went against your brother to protect me."

I touch the choker around her throat. "I told you I'd keep you safe."

"Because you own me?"

My gaze narrows. "Because you're mine."

She bites her lower lip, and those shadows in her gaze darken. "I want to tell you something, but I'm afraid."

Her body begins to tremble beneath my touch. Whatever's bothering her, it's serious. "Tell me."

"First, I need to know, am I still your enemy?"

It takes me a second to answer her. "That hasn't changed."

Just as quickly as the shadows came, they disappear behind a gray shuttered wall.

She glances at the clock on the nightstand which reads

nine thirty. "I should get ready. They're probably getting restless down there. Give me five minutes."

"I'll be downstairs."

Luca and Carina are already dressed and having breakfast in the dining room, and to my surprise, they've been joined by Gunn, Rowan, Noah, and his fiancée, Emily.

"Good morning," Carina says. "Sleep well?"

"Well enough."

"Help yourself to the bar. Nan made an amazing spread." She looks over at the older woman still setting up a buffet-style breakfast on the long table sitting by the windows.

"Thanks, but I'm not hungry." Then to Noah and Rowan, I say, "You two are here early."

"It's not a far drive for me," Noah says.

Rowan stabs three of the four sausage links on his plate. Out of everyone at the table, he's the largest, so it doesn't shock me that he prefers meat to anything else. "Luca texted me last night. I hopped on the first plane. Just got in."

"I messaged Gavin too, but he's not answering any of my calls," Luca says.

Noah's frowns. "I messaged him yesterday and he hasn't responded."

Luca taps a finger against the table. "Let's try again today. If there's still no answer, we'll make other calls. As far as anything we discuss here, we can fill him in later."

Nan pours something thick and green into a tall glass and drops it in front of Gunn. "Drink this."

"It looks like shit," he says.

She smacks the back of his head, and the sunglasses I

just noticed fall off his face. "And so do you. If you hadn't drunk the entire bottle of tequila, you wouldn't need that shit. And you." This is directed at Rowan. "Get some fruit on that plate. I don't care how fit you think you are, you can still die of a heart attack."

"Yes, ma'am."

Gunn rubs his temples. "You scare us, Nan."

"Good." As she grabs her purse from a nearby chair, she says to Luca, "I'm outta here before you all start discussing things I shouldn't hear."

"Bye, Nan. Love you!" Carina calls out as the woman leaves, then looks over at me. "Sit, Arran. You make me nervous standing over there like that."

I choose the seat next to her. "I spoke with Ruslan a bit ago. He has eyes on my house. As expected, it's surrounded by police."

"Oh, right to it," Carina says and takes a sip of orange juice. "I thought we could finish eating first."

"No time," I say. "I'd like to get there and see the damage for myself. I lost thirteen men."

"And you're sure it was Gideon?" Noah asks.

"There's no other possibility," I reply. "He's the only one who has anything to benefit from it."

Carina frowns, and I can see the wheels in her head spinning. "What about Skye?"

"What about her?" I ask.

"I know who she is, Arran. She seemed so familiar, I decided to do some digging last night. Turns out, I saw her face plastered all over the news a week or so ago when her father was killed. She's one of Thomas Cameron's daughters."

Noah's eyes snap to me. "Judge Thomas Cameron?"

"Oh yes, I heard about that," Emily says. "It was a really brutal murder at some fancy club."

"What is Thomas Cameron's daughter doing with you?" Noah asks.

I ignore him, focusing my attention on Carina. "What's your point?"

"My point is, the daughter of a judge who was literally gutted and displayed might have some enemies. And I think you're protecting her from those enemies."

Chancing a glance at Noah, I confirm the confusion and anger building behind his eyes. After all, why would the daughter of the man he killed on my order be under my protection?

"You're clever, Carina. You sure you don't want to work for me?"

Luca practically growls. "Keep your fucking offers to yourself, Maxton."

"Good morning." We all turn to see Skye standing in the doorway, wearing the light-blue shirt and black leggings Carina lent her. "Did I miss anything?"

"Only that everyone thinks one of your enemies blew up Arran's house," Gunn states matter-of-factly before he takes a swig of his green goo. "God, this shit is nasty."

"Uh..." Skye blinks nervously, obviously surprised at being the topic of conversation so soon.

Carina waves a hand in Gunn's direction. "Don't mind his gruff manner. He's usually better behaved. Why don't you grab something to eat and come join us?"

We all watch as she serves herself a plate of fruit and cheese. When she's done, I stand and extend my arm to her, encouraging her to sit beside me. "Skye, you met Luca and Carina last night. This hung-over mess is his first man,

Gunn. Beside him is Rowan, and that there is Noah and his girlfriend, Emily."

Emily is the only one who stands and offers a hand-shake, while Noah scowls at both Skye and me. "Pleased to meet you. I apologize for my fiancé. He's forgotten his manners too."

"Nice to meet everyone." Skye sets her plate down and sits. "So everyone thinks it's one of my enemies?"

"Who's after you, Skye? And why?" Rowan asks.

She pushes some of her cantaloupe around on her plate. "My father did have enemies. Men he owed money to. They think I have money."

"Do you?" Carina asks.

"No." Skye shakes her head and lifts her hands, palms up. "I don't have anything."

"Do you have any idea who killed your father?" Luca questions.

Noah chokes on a piece of bacon and we all turn to him. Emily slaps him on the back. "Are you all right?"

He nods as he takes a drink of water. "Just went down the wrong pipe."

Skye begins to become noticeably frazzled as the questions remain focused on her. "No. I have no idea who's come after us."

Rowan's brow furrows. "Us who?"

"She has a younger sister," I state. "Maisel."

"Maisie," she corrects. "But she's not a part of any of this."

"So it's just you?" Carina presses. "Where your sister?"

"She's safe. That's all anyone needs to know. And I'm not the one we need to be discussing here. No one but the people at Asta even know Arran bought my contract." She shoves a hunk of fruit into her mouth.

"At Asta?" Rowan whistles.

"You bought her?" Noah asks, still on the same line of questioning.

Emily gasps. "Like a slave?"

Skye swallows down her food loudly. "No. No. It's not like that," she defends. "I needed protection. So I sold my —" she cuts off, as if she's realized there's no good way to explain it. "I'm his, so he protects me."

"You fucking bought her?" Noah insists.

Finally having had enough, I slam my fist onto the table. "I had to, dammit!"

Everyone stares first at me, then at each other.

Carina clears her throat. "Whatever arrangement they have, it's their business. It has nothing to do with the alliance."

"I'm not a part of the alliance," I remind her.

"You are. Whether you want to be or not, you've become one of us," Luca says, leaving no room for argument. "Otherwise, you wouldn't have felt safe calling us in the middle of the night."

"Regardless, Skye is right. Very few people know that she was at Asta. It's unlikely any of her enemies do." I sit forward. "Gideon has been sending me letters asking for my father's location in exchange for my life. And last night, he was at Maxton House."

"That fuck was there and I've never even gotten an invite?" Rowan says. "Have any of you?"

"I have," Noah tells him, and Emily nods in agreement.

"Gideon wasn't invited!" I wipe a palm down my face. "It is the most secure location in the entire state, and he waltzes right the fuck in."

The table remains quiet as they all digest that. If he got into one of my places, what hope do they have?

It's Luca who finally breaks the silence. "You had him at your place and you let him go?"

I give him a look. "Don't go trying to break that down. You fuckers have fought him twice and he's still on the loose."

"Was he alone?" Luca asks.

"Yes."

"Do you know if any of your men betrayed you?" It's Carina's turn to speak.

"It must have been someone on the security team at Maxton House," Noah says.

"They could all be compromised," Rowan offers. "Have you shut down operations?"

"What about the security cameras?" Luca asks. "What did they capture?"

"Ruslan is going over the footage as we speak," I inform them.

"And your brother? Where is he? Has Gideon visited him too?" Again, Luca.

Questions are fired at me so fast that their voices begin to intermix and I can no longer tell them apart. The nerves in the back of my neck tense and I burst out, "What the fuck is this, an interrogation? It just happened last night. I need to get back to figure it all out."

The only sound that can be heard now is the clinking of Skye's fork as she sets it on her plate.

Then Gunn tilts back his green drink and chugs the rest of it before he wipes his mouth with the back of his arm and throws in a suggestion of his own. One that has us all turning in unison to Skye.

"Has anyone considered that maybe she has something to do with it?" he asks.

"That makes no sense," Emily says. "Unless she had access to the auction house herself, how could she have let Gideon in?"

Gunn groans and rubs his temples. "Yeah, sounded stupid even to my ears."

Carina taps the table with a finger as she observes Skye, but she says nothing. Simply watches her. And that is more telling to me than anything anyone could have said. She suspects Skye of something.

So I watch Skye carefully as I say, "Skye doesn't have access to any of my businesses. Just my home."

"And your bed." Carina only says three words, yet they're full of so much meaning.

Skye's breathing changes almost imperceptibly as she bores a hole into her plate with her gaze.

"Gideon has been a part of the black-market art scene for a while," Emily adds. "He had dealings with my father before we knew who he really was. So it's likely he would have already been familiar with Maxton House. I was. He could have been working on getting in for a long time."

"Would he have also been familiar with Asta?" Carina wonders.

"Wesley Ritter brought her contract to me, not Gideon," I tell her, still watching Skye. And she still doesn't look up.

Luca narrows his gaze. "How do you know Ritter doesn't work for Black?"

I can't answer the question, because the truth is, I don't. Wes is a very well-connected man. It's not out of the realm of possibility that he'd have run into Gideon at some point. But I simply never had a reason to put those two things together.

"What does the contract say?" Carina asks.

"That I'll provide protection in exchange for anything I want from her."

"Anything?" Gunn whistles. "Damn."

"What about money?" Carina continues her line of questioning. "Was she getting money?"

"Money?" I frown.

"Do you think she's being blackmailed?" Luca asks.

"Stop talking about me like I'm not here!" Skye shouts, slamming her palms onto the table as she stands. "You're trying to figure out something that isn't possible to because of how fucking ludicrous it is!" She drops her face into her hands and sighs.

"Are you involved with Gideon?" Carina pushes.

"I didn't let him into the club, if that's what you're asking."

"It's not."

Skye lifts her gaze and sighs again, and, suddenly, it all makes sense. Why someone would choose to sell herself at Asta when it's not a kink. Why her eyes searched the room wildly as she was being auctioned but settled on me the moment they locked with mine. And why she was so afraid of Gideon when he showed up. Only, it wasn't fear of him. It was fear of being discovered.

"Gideon set me up," I speak the last thought that passes through my mind. "It wasn't me you sold yourself to. It was him all along. You sold yourself to him in exchange for protection."

"Not *my* protection." She looks at me, her gray eyes wide and pleading. "He has my sister."

I stand too, anger and jealousy rising in my chest at the thought of what Skye might have done with Gideon. "So, what? He sent you to me as a spy in return for your safety?"

"It wasn't about me," she retorts. "I don't give a damn about myself. I have to tell him where your father is, or he will kill Maisie!"

"Oh God." Emily leans into Noah, and he wraps an arm around her.

I'm nose-to-nose with Skye, our gazes locked in silent communication even as we speak with words. "So you'd have him kill my father instead?"

"It's not like that."

"Then please explain to me what it's like?"

She wipes at a wayward tear and straightens her spine. "My back is pinned to the wall, Arran. I don't want anyone else to die. Tell me you'd have done anything different for your sister."

Sarcastic laughter bursts from me. "I understand. You had a choice to make. Now I do too." Before she can react, I snatch the collar from her throat.

"Arran!" Crying out, her hand slaps the red line on her skin where the diamonds sat.

"You're free."

19

SKYE

I'm free.

Only, my freedom isn't the kind most people seek. It's not a gift. And if it is, it comes wrapped up in a pretty death sentence.

Arran knew what he was condemning me to when he so harshly tore the collar I've been wearing for eight days.

I spread balm over the red welt on my neck, wincing when it burns. Barely a week, and I grew accustomed to the weight of it. To the way it touched me all day and night. A constant reminder of my indenture to Arran.

Now it's gone, and, somehow, I'm not sure what stings more. The mark or the absence of the diamonds.

"Skye, are you all right in there?" Carina calls through the bathroom door.

I turn from the mirror. "I'll be right out."

After the disaster at the breakfast table, Arran and the other men adjourned to Luca's study. It was Carina's idea to separate us. Maybe she was afraid Arran would do more than tear off the choker. But he's not the type to hurt a woman. In bed, sure. But not in violence. Though I'm not sure there was anything more punishing than taking his protection away when he's fully aware of the consequences.

We came up to my room and I told her and Emily everything. It all just sort of bubbled out of me desperately, starting with the day Maisie and I tried to run and ending with the bomb going off. All the while, I reached for the collar that wasn't there but I'd grown so accustomed to.

Mistaking it for discomfort, Carina gave me the salve her housekeeper makes and instructed me to put it on the wound to help with the pain. I didn't tell her that it wasn't the soreness that had me touching my throat constantly. I didn't say that the thing had become a security blanket for me. Yes, it was a reminder that I was owned. But it also meant I was protected. Safe.

When I step out of the bathroom, they're waiting for me, sitting on the bed that just last night, I shared with Arran.

I shake my head to dispel the images of our bodies entwined, him inside me. The last kiss we shared.

"Come." Emily pats the spot between them. "Let's talk."

"I think I'd rather stand."

"We won't bite," Carina jokes.

I glance at the bed sadly. "It's not that."

"Oh. I understand." Emily's blue eyes fill with compassion, and I can tell she truly does understand. "The enemy squirmed his way into your heart. Happens to the best of us."

Carina huffs. "Fucking men." She stands and grabs me by the arms. "You can pine over him later. Right now, you need to figure out what you're going to do next."

"Do you have anywhere else to go?" Emily asks.

"No. Besides, it doesn't matter if I can find a place to

hide. Maisie is still being held prisoner." I worry my lower lip. "God, the place she was in was a dungeon."

Tears well up in my eyes. Emily comes to us and offers me a handkerchief. I wipe them, only to have them spring again.

Carina moves away and begins pacing as she taps her chin in thought. "If you knew where Arran's father was, you could get her freed."

"Are you suggesting she betray Arran?" Emily seems aghast and intrigued at the same time.

"Betray what? He's pretty much set her on the street, knowing she'd be a sitting duck. So to speak. I mean, you're welcome to stay here as long as you want to, and Luca would have to give his protection or he'll have to deal with me." She winks.

"Me too," Emily declares. "If you want to come to Jersey with Noah and me, that is."

I give them a grateful smile. "Thanks. But I wouldn't want to cause trouble. And you guys need Arran in the alliance. He won't do that if I'm around."

"So then what?" Carina continues her pacing. "Do you have any ideas where Arran might be hiding Clive? I've discovered the last two places, but—"

"Maxton House," I blurt. "He's at Maxton House."

Carina stops and looks at me with utter confusion, her brows pinched so tightly together, they look like one slash across her forehead. "Where in Maxton House?"

"Underground. There are offices and other facilities down there. I saw a nurse coming out of a room with pills and food. Immediately, I knew that's where he is." But I pretended not to. Deep down, I knew it the instant I saw that woman, but I looked the other way because Arran had just saved me from getting raped.

"Wait a minute." Carina lifts a finger, her mind working. "But I've gone over the blueprints for Maxton House. There's nothing about an underground."

Emily wrinkles her nose. "Why are you going over the blueprints? And how did you even get them?"

"I wanted something to hold over Arran. Show him that if I can find Clive's location, so could Gideon. It was supposed to be a hard nudge into agreeing to join the alliance." She grins. "But he's even smarter than I thought."

"You scare me sometimes, Carina," Emily says.

"So he's at the auction house. That means you go to Gideon and tell him exactly that. Get your sister and run."

I think back to everything Arran and I shared over the last week. About his threats and hatred of my father. I also recall the way he made me feel. How protective he's been, to the point where he's shielded me with his own body.

He's an enigma that confuses my senses and I can't be sure if I hate him or I...

"All this time, I've wanted nothing more than to save my sister. I now have the ability to, and I'm hesitating because of Arran, even after what he's done," I say. "Because it will gut him all over again, and there's no telling if Gideon will stop there. What if he kills Arran too?"

And there it is, spoken aloud. My real fear that Arran will pay the ultimate price. The women glance at each other but say nothing.

"What does that say about me?" I ask.

"It says you fell for the ass," Carina tells me sadly. "It says life is fucking unfair when it makes you choose between two people you love."

"So what do I do?"

"You save your sister," she says with vehemence. "Let us

handle saving Clive. Whatever plans Gideon has for him, they're not going to be immediate."

"Arran won't agree." Why would he? Now he sees me as a traitorous spy on top of being the daughter of the man who murdered his sister.

"He won't know until it's too late," she retorts. "The question is, how are you supposed to contact Gideon?"

"I'm supposed to go to a warehouse right outside of Philly. It's empty, but he has cameras. When I show up, so will a driver." I repeat the address he forced me to memorize by turning it into a stupid little tune. "That means I have to go alone."

"I figured that much. It will be imperative that we don't attack too soon, but we can only wait so long." Carina tugs her phone from her pocket. "You take this. Em and I will be in touch with you as long as we can. I'm sure that once you arrive, Gideon will have you searched."

"How will I get there?"

She wraps an arm around my shoulders and guides me to the door. "You'll take one of our cars. A mile before you reach your destination, pull over and call me. Then find a place where you can hide the phone. If you can go back to that location, you'll still have a means of communication.

"When I get that call, I'll set a timer for one hour. The first thing Gideon will do is confirm what you're telling him. Once he does, he might want to hold on to you for insurance. I don't care what you have to do, Skye, but you need to get away. Promise him the world, I don't care. Be gone as fast as you can."

I cover my face with my hands and dig my fingers into my eye sockets. "I was just supposed to be a lawyer."

"Then use your argument skills to get out of there." She paces to the bed and back, drawing up her plan in her mind. "Once you call me, I'll wait an hour and then let the men know what's happening. The first thing Arran will do is have his father moved. So I don't know how you need to do it, but you and Maisie have to be gone by the time Gideon discovers Clive is no longer at Maxton House."

I inhale deeply, then exhale slowly, doing my best to calm my nerves. "Okay."

"Where will you go after?" Emily asks.

"There's a house in Vermont. No one knows about it but Maisie and me."

"Do you have money?" Emily asks.

Nodding, I reply, "Cash. In the duffel bag I packed before Gideon captured us. He has the bag, but he agreed to return it when he frees Maisie."

"Just in case..." Carina disappears down the hall, and when she returns, she hands me five hundred dollars and a credit card. "Shove that into your pants. If Gideon takes the car and your money, you can use this to get transportation."

The thoughtful gesture touches me and I hug her. "Thank you."

"Make sure you're not being followed before you leave," she tells me. "And call us if you need anything."

The girls walk me down the stairs, flanking me. It makes me wish for more time with them. I bet we would be good friends, and I need more of those.

As we move through the foyer, the sound of men's voices can be heard loud and clear. They're arguing, not shouting necessarily, but the tone is heated.

"This isn't the time or the place for this conversation. It isn't Sinacore business," Luca booms.

But he's obviously ignored when who I believe is Noah says, "It's not Sinacore business, but it is mine. Her father's blood is on my hands, on your fucking orders, and you're fucking her?"

All three of us freeze just outside the dining room doors.

"I'm not fucking her anymore," Arran says. "And what you did for me was a favor you agreed to. A no-questions-asked favor. Or have you forgotten already?"

"I wish I could fucking forget," Noah growls. "You told me he killed your sister. I'd never have my sister's murderer in my bed."

"You certainly didn't have a problem fucking Emily when you thought her father had killed yours." Arran's voice lowers. "Or am I recalling that wrong?"

I turn to Emily, who's standing there with her hand clasped over her mouth, her skin a deep shade of red. "Noah killed my father?"

Her brilliant blue eyes go wide as she stares at me. "Oh my God. I had no idea, Skye. He never said anything about it to me."

"Of course he wouldn't," I grit through my teeth, anger beginning to rise from the pit of my belly. It cuts through all the confusion and allows me to see clearly. "It was business to him. A favor owed to Arran. But *I* should have known better."

"Did you suspect it?" Carina asks.

My face snaps to hers at the realization that, yes, I suspected it. Tears burn in my eyes, part pain, part anger, and all shame. Because, in the beginning, I asked him. And I chose to believe him when he said he didn't touch Daddy.

"I have to go," I say. "Now."

Carina gives me a curt nod. Then, as one, the three of us head to the garage. The guards don't question us as we move quickly past them. They don't even blink as I climb into one of three black SUVs and turn on the ignition.

"Remember, stop a mile before you get to the place and call me. You'll have an hour before I rile up the men. Once they learn what you've done, they'll want to get Clive out fast. But they'll also come after you." Carina reaches in through the window and squeezes my hand. "Go save your sister for the both of us."

I don't understand what she means by saving Maisie for her too, but I nod anyway. Then with all hesitation at giving up Arran's beloved father gone, I step on the gas and make my way to Gideon.

20

SKYE

I've never thought of myself as weak. Sure, I've had weaknesses. Areas I could improve on. But I've always believed my strengths more than made up for that. I'm smart. Brave. Loyal.

And yet none of those things are helping me now. What does being smart do for me when I can't think of a way to avoid someone's death? And did I say loyal? Where was my loyalty when I hesitated after discovering Clive's location because I knew his death would hurt a man who despises me?

Brave? All I can do is laugh through the tears as I make my way back to Pennsylvania, my arms trembling so hard, it's tough to control the steering wheel. I'm scared of everything right now.

My emotions are all over the place. Fear, pain from betrayal, shame for not wanting to hurt Arran when all I should have cared about was Maisie. That any feelings I might have for him made me stumble, and I hate myself for it!

Weak. I'm weak on far too many levels.

They say you should give yourself grace. Remember that you're only human. I don't have the time for that luxury right now.

What I need is rage at Arran and at myself to fuel me. To give me the power I lack in this weakened state to do what I have to.

It works, and I slam my foot against the pedal and go up ten miles per hour. Faster, but not so fast that a cop will pull me over. A traffic stop isn't something I can afford right now.

As I fly down the interstate, I imagine how angry Arran will be with me. How angry they will *all* be with Carina and Emily for keeping my exit a secret.

Then I imagine them working together as the alliance Luca and Carina want. A powerful well-oiled machine that could get to Clive before Gideon lets us go. If that happens, Maisie and I are dead.

Shit.

I'm a mile from the TK Warehouse, parked behind a convenience store, staring down at the phone. The moment I call, the timer will be set in motion.

I climb out of the SUV and hide the phone under one of the dumpsters. It looks pretty empty, so with luck, the waste department won't be back for a few days.

"I'm sorry," I whisper to the wind. I'm sorry, but I can't risk Maisie's life anymore. I'm sorry if this costs a man his life. I'm sorry that Arran will possibly hate me even more than I hate *him* at this moment.

Arran believes Daddy had his sister killed. Now he'll think I killed his father. He'll likely want revenge for that too. But that's a worry for another day.

I get back into the vehicle and brace myself for what comes next.

The warehouse is located on the outskirts of town, on a street where most of the businesses are manufacturers or sell building supplies. It's not a very busy place. In fact, I only pass three cars on the way.

I pull into the parking lot and drive around the building as I was instructed, stopping just outside a cargo door in the back. Although there's no sign of anyone being around, I get the sense of being watched.

Scanning the area, I see why. High, on each rooftop corner and over the three entrances visible, there are cameras. And they're all directed at me, the red flashing lights indicating they're on.

Straightening my spine, I wait. Ten minutes later, a black Bentley arrives, coming around to park beside me. When I glance through the rearview mirror, I realize that two black SUVs have also shown up. One pulls up right behind me, the other, on my passenger side, completely blocking me in.

Several men dressed in suits step out of their vehicles and stand in that position guards always tend to get in, with their legs spread shoulder-width apart and their hands clasped in front of them. They're armed too and make no attempt at hiding the gun hilts poking through their coats or hanging from their belts.

Once they're in place, Gideon emerges from the Bentley, dressed to kill in a powder-blue button-up shirt rolled up at the sleeves and black slacks, looking very much like the billionaire devil he is. It surprises me to see him, because I would have assumed it'd be too risky. He comes to my door and opens it. A grins spreads over his handsome face when he sees me. "Imogen, so nice to see you. It took you long enough."

"It's Skye."

"Ah, yes, Skye. I apologize." He extends his hand to me and assists me down from the high seat. Then he makes a gesture to one of his men.

The bulky guard stands behind me and begins to pat me down. First my arms, then my legs and back. When he's satisfied that there's nothing on me, he searches the car.

"I wasn't expecting *you* to show up," I tell him. "Figured you'd meet me at that dingy hole you're keeping my sister in."

He laughs. "It's not that dingy. Besides, I knew you wouldn't try to trick me. You're too clever for that. That, and I'm sure that by now, you've figured out who murdered your father?"

I narrow my gaze on his. "What do you know about that?"

His steel-blue eyes glitter with amusement. "Noah is good, but he fucked up. A camera *did* capture his profile. I had it deleted, of course. The game wouldn't be as fun if he was behind bars."

"A picture of Noah isn't enough to prove it had anything to do with Arran," I argue pointlessly.

"No. But don't forget that I've been a part of this game a lot longer than you have. I can see all the puzzle pieces from my position."

The guard comes around the car. "It's clean, boss."

"Good. Now shall we go? I'm dying to know everything you've learned about Clive's whereabouts."

I dig my heels in when he tries to guide me toward the Bentley. "You're taking me to where Maisie is, right?"

"Yes. We're going directly to that dingy hole I'm

keeping her in. On the way, you're going to talk." He opens the door for me and I slide onto the buttery-soft leather seat.

It takes every ounce of strength I possess not to run out as he rounds the hood and gets in himself. The engine roars to life, powerful and intimidating, just like the man beside me.

One of the SUVs goes ahead of us. Then a minute later, Gideon gets a message on his cell phone, which I assume is the all clear, and we move, the other vehicle following behind us.

"So tell me, how has your time with Arran been?" he asks. "I was glad to see he hadn't killed you."

I shake my head in annoyance. "Did you go to the club to warn Arran? Or was it for me?"

"Both?" He chuckles. "Truthfully, I was just in the area and wanted to have a little fun."

Like a cat toying with its food.

"Your little fun could have ruined everything." God, I was so nervous, I thought I'd vomit. "Arran could have discovered me and you'd still have no idea where Clive is."

"Speaking of which, where exactly did you say he was?"

"I didn't. And I won't until I see that Maisie is safe."

"Fair enough."

I stare ahead, watching as we enter the city, the road becoming more and more congested. "Has she asked for me?"

"Not really." He shrugs.

A knot forms in my throat as I picture her in that basement we were held in, the walls made of cinder block, not a window in sight. There was a cot, the sort one takes camping, so at least I don't believe she's been sleeping on the floor. But our things were taken. Her precious sketchbook.

Has she been treated decently? Fed? Allowed to see the sun at all?

All of these questions are flowing through my mind when we pull up to a swanky building not far from where Maxton House is located.

"Where are we?" I ask, glancing all around us.

"Well, your sister's temporary prison, of course."

I frown. "What?"

A valet comes around the Bentley just as Gideon steps out. "Take good care of her."

"Yes, sir."

Another man opens the door for me. I exit the car in somewhat of a stupor and take Gideon's arm when he offers it. "This isn't where we were before."

"Oh, that?" He shivers dramatically. "I'd never have kept a lady there. Too many rats. That was just in case you needed motivation."

"So she's here?"

"Why else would I bring you here? I'm anxious to get Clive. Believe me, I'm the last person who would prolong this. Besides, Scar might be ready to kill your sister by now. She's not the kid type."

"Who's Scar?"

As we walk into the beautiful reception area that reminds me of an upscale hotel, I imagine Maisie dealing with this woman who doesn't like kids. Was she horrible to her? God, I just need to see her already.

There are four elevators in the lobby. Several people hop onto the first one that opens. I try to as well, but Gideon stops me.

"Wait," he says, holding his arm out to keep me from moving.

When another one opens, a tall Asian man peers out.

He's just as handsome as Gideon, dressed just as deadly gorgeous. And when they make eye contact, I realize he's one of his guards.

After we enter, he stands menacingly at the doors, preventing anyone else from approaching.

Gideon presses the button for the ninth floor. The elevator ascends rapidly and delivers us to a long hallway lined with doors with pretty wreaths and golden numbers.

But it's not the doors that get my attention. It's the many cameras stationed at intervals throughout.

The guard goes ahead of us and knocks on the door at the very end of the hall. A blonde woman opens it.

"Itsuki," she greets. Then she glances over his shoulder at us. "Ah, you're here so soon."

The guard leans in and whispers something in her ear, then she nods, dismissing him.

"Scar, this is Imo— I mean Skye," Gideon introduces. "Skye, this is Scarlet. She's my..."

"I'm your number one," she offers when he seems stuck for words. "The underboss."

"She's Maisel's babysitter," he says with a huge grin.

Her red lips tug to one side and she crosses her arms. "You know, Giddy, you're starting to annoy me."

His smile fades. "I see the girl is rubbing off on you." He reaches over and touches a thin red cut on her cheek. "What the fuck happened to you? Did you fight someone without telling me?"

"Training." Moving aside, she indicates for us to enter. After checking the hallway, she shuts the door and engages five locks.

"You have enemies to worry about?" I ask.

"Not as many as you," she replies.

"I want to see my sister." I push past the foyer into the

lovely home. "Maisie!" When she doesn't answer right away, I call for her again, "Maisie!"

I move fast through every room I come across, searching for her. Somewhere in the distance, I hear a muffled, "Skye?"

Running toward it, I find myself in the kitchen, where I freeze, completely dumbfounded by the sight before me. Maisie, takeout Chinese spread out on the table, noodles hanging from her mouth, and a magazine in front of her.

She scrambles out of her seat, wiping away hair that has strayed from her messy bun. "Skye! You're here!"

Our bodies collide, my arms wrapping around her so tight, I'm afraid I'll asphyxiate her, but I can't help it.

"Maze, I missed you so much!" I cup her cheeks and examine every speck on her face, searching for signs of injury. "Are you okay? Have you been hurt?"

"No. I'm fine. What about you? Did that pig who bought you treat you well?"

"Well enough." I hug her again, noticing how clean she smells and the nice clothes she's wearing. "Where did you get these?"

"Scarlet got us matching pajamas."

"I mean, I wasn't trying to be twins or anything," the woman says sheepishly. "I just liked them too."

Turning my attention back to my sister, I ask, "So they didn't keep you in that basement at all?"

She shakes her head. "Nah. Like five minutes after you left, so did we. I've been here with Scarlet ever since."

I glance at Scarlet with her matching pajamas. "And she's treated you well?"

"Really well. We've been having a lot of fun."

Taking both her hands, I squeeze them. "Maisie, I was so afraid something was going to happen to—" I pause as my thumbs come across bandages. When I peer down, I see that her knuckles have been wrapped.

She tries to pull away, but I grasp the wrist of one arm at the same time that I tug up the sleeve. Her arm is covered in small scrapes and bruises and I gasp in horror.

"It's not what you think!" Maisie manages to free herself and quickly covers the injuries.

"Then exactly what is it?" I place myself protectively between my sister and the two killers in the room.

"Scarlet's been teaching me to fight."

Gideon turns to his female lackey. "Is that what we're doing now, Scar? Teaching our captives how to fight back?"

"I was just teaching her self-defense. It's not like she can use any of it against me."

He pinches her chin and turns her face so that he can get a better view of that slash across her cheek. "Was this in self-defense? I can't recall another time when someone has been able to get close to your face."

She slaps his hand away. "Sometimes you have to let someone think they're winning."

"You let me win?" Maisie's tone is full of disappointment.

"There shouldn't have been a fight to win in the first place," I say.

"Enough with the chitchat. You can catch up later." Gideon goes to sit on one of the plush ivory couches in the living room and we follow. "As you can see, Maisel is doing fine. She even got some martial arts lessons out of it."

"It's freaking Maisie!" My little sister turns beet red. "Maisie, dammit."

He ignores her. Motioning for me to sit beside him, he says, "It's time for you to tell me where the fuck Clive Maxton is."

"First, swear that you will let us go. That once we step out those doors, you will not seek us out. And our debts will be paid to anyone searching for us. It's what you promised."

"And I never go back on my word. I swear it."

I bite my lower lip, still feeling that damned hesitation to hurt Arran. My beautiful Arran, who owned me in so many ways, and still... I still want him.

My lips part and both Gideon and Scarlet sit forward, their attention captured. "He's beneath Maxton House. Underground."

His blue gaze narrows. "Impossible. There is no underground."

"There is," I assure him. "Apparently, Arran is a lot smarter than you think."

The glare he gives me is hot enough to singe the hair right off my head. "You'll stay here until I can confirm it's true. If you're lying—"

"I'm not."

He leans into me. "If you're lying, I'll kill you. But not before I torture and kill your little sister while you watch. That will be fun, won't it, Scar?"

Maisie gasps and looks pleadingly at Scarlet. "You'd do that?"

Scarlet doesn't reply to either of them. Instead, she points a harsh finger at me. "You better not be lying."

"I'm not."

Gideon stares at her so intensely, it speaks volumes. He wasn't expecting that. I'd bet almost anything she's always the obedient guard dog. But not today. However, he doesn't address it.

To me, he says, "Stay here. I'll be back in a few."

He locks himself in one of the rooms, leaving the three of us to wait for him. Maisie comes to sit next to me on the sofa, and I wrap my arms around her again, so happy she's safe. "I've been so worried about you. All I could do was hope that I'd see you again."

"How was that man you were sent to? Was he cruel?" she asks.

I want to tell her that, yes, he was very cruel at the beginning. At the end too. But the in-between was filled with something else entirely. Lust, pleasure like I've never experienced before. Then there were the small moments where we became something undefined. Like bonded enemies, hating each other yet wanting to live inside the other's skin.

But that's too much to say, especially to a fifteen-year-old girl. Instead, I smile and pat her shoulder. "I was treated well." Over her head, I spy Scarlet watching us curiously. "And her? How was she to you?"

Scarlet huffs. "I tortured her every day. Beat her and starved her."

"Shh. She's going to believe you," Maisie hisses at her. Then to me, she says, "She was a perfect hostess, actually. Treated me like a big sister would."

"A big sister?" I laugh. Jesus, looks like we both got struck with Stockholm syndrome. "I'm your only sister, Maze. Don't get whatever kindness she showed you twisted." The remark comes out tinged with a bit of jealousy, and I really hope she doesn't notice.

Unfortunately, the grin that spreads over Scarlet's face tells me *she* does. "We had fun, didn't we, kid?" she asks, but her green eyes remain on me. "Maybe we can hang out again sometime."

I bite back a nasty retort. I love Maisie, but for her, a hard no would be too tempting not to rebel against.

Gideon returns and sits on the coffee table in front of

me. "Well, it appears you're right. There is an underground level."

"I fulfilled my end of the bargain. Now it's your turn. Let Maisie and me go."

Amusement fills his expression. "You're too smart to believe I'd do that. First, I want you to tell me exactly how you got into that underground. Every detail you recall."

"If you already have confirmation the place is there, you also know how to get in."

"On paper, yes." He leans in. "I want a first-hand account."

"I tell you where he is. You let us go. That was the deal," I remind him.

"Didn't anyone ever tell you not to make deals with the devil?" His smile widens, making him appear devilish indeed. "Make yourself comfortable. You're not going anywhere until I've put a bullet in Clive's head. And if you try anything, I'll put one in yours too."

21

ARRAN

The tension in the room is palpable. Noah fumes at the fact that the daughter of the man he so viciously killed is under the same roof. Even though he did something similar, he can't comprehend the possibility of my sharing a bed with her if everything I said about Thomas Cameron is true.

Frankly, neither can I. But there are many things in life I can't understand.

Luca has been playing mediator for the last hour while Rowan shakes his head and grumbles his regret at having come at all. Gunn is the only one oblivious to anything that's going on, happily snoring away on the long leather couch.

"All this proves is that Gideon is a threat to all of us." Luca moves to the wet bar and pours whiskey into four glasses and hands them to us, keeping one for himself. "You're already in the thick of it, Arran. He's focusing all of his energy on finding Clive right now."

"Perhaps it's just a trick. Noah is the new Gianni Don. What's to say he won't come after him again? Or you,

Rowan?" I point at the Boston mobster who's now running the McKenzie gang.

"I haven't made any official claims. Gideon has no idea I'm the boss."

I smile. "He penetrated Maxton House. Do you really think he's doesn't know you're in charge?"

"We're not stupid," Luca interjects. "Gideon can come after any of us at any time. That's why we've joined forces. Together, we're stronger."

A chuckle escapes me and I take a sip, savoring the amber liquid. Then I look at each of them. "And what happens when it ends? When Gideon is dead, will you still be best friends? As I recall, Jersey and New York were battling for territory not that long ago?"

Noah and Luca glance at each other, and it's obvious they've had similar thoughts.

"It's possible we'll go back to the same thing," Luca says. "I never promised eternal friendship. Just a temporary truce." Walking around his desk, he plops into his chair. He lets out a long sigh, and for the first time, I notice the weariness in his expression.

"A truce," I whisper, testing the word.

"The truth is, Arran, we need each other. Gideon has already taken some of us out. Now he has my sister, and I can't pin that fucker down. He's everywhere and nowhere." The hand he has on the desk forms a tight fist and his jaw clenches. It takes him a moment as he regains control. "Whether we like it or not, we fucking need each other."

I nod reluctantly. The asshole is right. Even if I can hold off Gideon a bit longer, I can't forever.

"Fine. I'll join the alliance. But when this is over, it's over."

Luca raises his glass to me. "To partnerships with expiration dates."

Without bothering to knock, Carina slides open the pocket doors and walks in, followed closely by a nervous-looking Emily.

Immediately, Luca's gaze narrows as he takes in his wife's demeanor. "What's the matter?"

"We have a problem."

"What kind of a problem?" he asks.

Both Carina and Emily glare at me, letting me know that whatever the issue is, it has to do with Skye.

"Where is she?" I demand.

"You gave her no choice." The way she hisses, she clearly blames me.

"Where is she?" I repeat.

"She left."

She left? No goodbyes? No last words? Just left?

Not that I would have expected anything different. Wanted anything different. In fact, I never want to see her again.

And yet the idea of her out there unarmed, trying to save her sister on her own, makes my stomach clench.

I move to peer out the window. "Did she say where she was going?"

"Where the hell else would she go? She went to see Gideon."

Her words are like a punch to the gut. I whirl at the same time as Luca growls, "Gideon? She knows where Gideon is and you let her go?"

"Not only did I let her go, but I gave her one of our trucks."

Luca shakes his head. "She could have helped us get to him! To Sofia!"

"Like she would have done that after she overheard Noah and Arran."

"What did she overhear?" I ask the women.

"That Noah killed Skye's father," Emily says accusingly. "On your order."

"It's not what you think," Noah says to her pleadingly.

"We'll talk about it later." She tugs out of his grasp when he tries to hold her.

Luca grinds his teeth, his scowl intense as he goes to his wife. He towers over her, but she doesn't budge. "The fucker has my sister. Any chance we have to get her back, we have to take it, Carina. Dammit!"

"And that bitch of his killed mine. Or have you forgotten that?" she retorts. "But it's not about Sofia or Alma right now. It's about a fifteen-year-old girl who's probably scared shitless."

I walk away from the couple arguing and wipe a palm down my face in frustration as my other hand wraps around the diamond collar tucked in my pocket. Fuck me, I should have known that the moment this came off, Skye would do something stupid. I'm not sure if I want to punish her for putting herself at risk or myself for letting her believe she could.

"He's going to kill her," I say through gritted teeth. "Goddammit, he's going to kill them both."

"It's not just her you need to worry about." The ominous tone in Carina's voice has me turning to her. "It's your father."

———

You've guaranteed Skye's failure. All she wanted was to protect her little sister. Out of the kindness of my heart, I'll delay their death sentence. Bring me your father by seven, and I'll spare them.

I read the message and address that was sent from an unknown number. Asshole obviously got a hold of one of my business cards.

Luca glances at me through the rearview mirror of his SUV. "What is it?"

"It appears Gideon just learned my father was moved out of Maxton House." I turn to look out at the passing scenery. "Fuck!" I slam a fist against the door.

After Carina informed us that Skye did in fact go to Gideon, armed with the knowledge of where Father is, I chided myself for forgetting how smart she is. How those big gray eyes aren't haunting at all. They're cunning.

The entire time she was with me, she was on high alert for any sign of his whereabouts like a good little spy. But not good enough.

Father has been moved to a location provided by Luca. A random place that will keep him out of Gideon's grasp long enough for us to pick him up and bring him back to Briar House. He's safe.

She's not. I shut off the voice in my head. Block out the image of her on the bed this morning.

"I want to tell you something, but I'm afraid," she'd said.

Was she going to tell me she was a spy? Was she going to ask for help but changed her mind because you don't beg the enemy for mercy?

The enemy who swore to protect her.

Ignoring that thought, I ask, "What is this place?" when we arrive at a building in Queens.

Luca tugs his gun from the center console and pulls back on the slide, checking the chamber. He hands it to me.

"Gunn and I used to live here. I still own the building, but it's unlikely Gideon would think of this place."

I inspect the Glock. Usually, I'm surrounded by an armed entourage. And when I'm alone, I depend on my knife for self-protection. Firearms aren't my weapon of choice, but with Gideon around, I may need it.

Gunn and I step out of the first SUV, the one driven by Luca. Rowan and Noah are in the vehicle behind us. The plan is to get Father from Ruslan, who's meeting us at this address.

Should something have gone wrong and this is all a trap, we have men located at several street corners, all facing the building.

Gunn leads the way through the back door, and we ascend via a stairwell, quickly and quietly, to the fifth floor.

"Welcome to the penthouse." Gunn grins as he raps on the door.

Ruslan greets us, letting us pass only after he's peeked down the hall to make sure we weren't followed. "Boss."

"How was it?" I ask, looking over his shoulder at my father.

"He's not happy. But he's alive."

While I'd hardly call it a penthouse, it is a nice enough space. Clean pine floors, white kitchenette, and a few furnishings. Like the couch Father is sitting on, sulking, with a sour-faced Martha by his side.

She cocks her head when she sees me. "You know I'm not getting paid enough for this shit."

"Tomorrow I'll double your pay."

Her expression smooths a bit. "Fine. Okay."

"Will you wait for us outside?" I ask her.

She nods and is taken to the waiting vehicles by Gunn.

I go to crouch in front of my father so that I'm not

towering over him threateningly and take his fragile hand in mine. "Father, how are you feeling?"

"Why am I here?!" he demands without paying any mind to the other men in the room. "Do you have any idea how many times you've moved me now?"

"Do *you*?" I rebuke.

"Eight."

"Ah shit, he *is* keeping track." Ruslan whistles.

"Father, it's the only way to keep you safe from Gideon. Do you remember Gideon? Stephen Black's son?"

As he always does when I mention the name, he shakes his head uncontrollably. "He's dead and I don't want this anymore. Let me go, Arran. I beg you."

"Stephen is dead. But Gideon is very much alive and he'll kill you. He wants revenge for what you did. Do you remember what you did?"

"We did what had to be done!"

"I know you did. But he still wants revenge."

"I don't care! I want to die." Sobs begin to wrack his body. It's the same conversation. Same damn words he always uses.

I stand, frustration roiling through my veins. "Have you any idea of the shit I've been through to protect you, Father? The things I've done?"

"Let him kill me! I deserve to die. Kate. Kate!"

"Why do you keep saying that? If you did what you had to, why do you deserve to die?" I yell, tired of this. Tired of everything. "Kate's gone. She's been gone for two years. But I'm still here, taking care of you. Taking care of everything you made."

Tears roll down his wrinkled cheeks as he looks right through me. "Kate."

I try to swallow the anger that forms in the base of my

throat. Nothing will ever bring Kate back for him. Not the drugs. Not the crying and begging for her to return.

The only thing he doesn't have is closure. Revenge.

"Thomas Cameron is dead," I finally tell him.

"Judge Cameron?" he whispers.

"I killed him."

"He's dead?" His thin lips part and his eyes widen in horror. Now, he does see me, and I almost wish he didn't. "You killed him?"

"I had to, Father. He was behind Kate's death."

"You killed him after I begged you not to?" The question is laced with disbelief.

"Yes. Kate had to be avenged."

"You swore to me you wouldn't touch him!" He tries to stand, but his knees are too weak and he falls back onto the couch. Staring at his palms, he cries, "There's so much blood on my hands!"

"I don't understand, Father. Why would you want the man who murdered your daughter alive?!"

"Don't you see, boy? I don't. I want Kate's murderer dead. But *you*"—he jams a finger in my direction—"won't let me die!"

I rear back as if he punched me. "What?"

"It was me, Arran! I did it. I killed Kate." Again, he attempts to stand, and this time, he manages it, powered by a mix of rage and pain. "You refuse to let me die when it's all I've wanted for two damned years!"

"What are you saying, Father?"

He falls to his knees at my feet and sobs like a child. Wiping the tears from his eyes on the back of his arm, he peers up at me imploringly. As if he's begging me to understand. Begging me for forgiveness. "Yegor came to the house that day because I hired him. Kelly wanted a divorce and was holding the affair I had with Barb over my head. She would have taken everything! So I hired him. But when I sent him the photo, I..." A wail of sheer sorrow emerges from him like the sound of a tortured soul. "I accidentally sent him Kate's picture."

The horror at what he says has me staring at him in shock, my mouth parted on a scream that won't come out.

"Oh shit," Rowan and Ruslan both say at the same time.

I stumble back until I hit the wall behind me. And even then, all I can do is look at him. But I'm not seeing him at all. The only thing I see is Kate's broken body on the steps where Yegor dumped her. And Thomas Cameron, the innocent man I condemned to a humiliating death.

And Skye.

I left her without her guardian. I made her pay for a crime not even her father was guilty of. I rejected her for doing what she had to in order to protect her little sister.

"Forgive me," Father whispers.

The hate that's been brewing inside me, a churning toxic brew, erupts. Before I know what I'm doing, his shirt is in my fists and I'm nose-to-nose with him. "I killed Skye's father because of you!"

"I begged you not to!"

"Arran! We must go." Ruslan tries to pry me from Father, but I'm too angry.

It's only when my own fault in all of this hits that I release him. He begged me not to. It was me who couldn't stop. Me who ordered the hit.

And I'm the only one who can fix it.

Gently, I release the tight grip on his shirt. I wrap my arm around his shoulders and place my chin on his head.

My chest made tight from the myriad of emotions slamming into me, I say, "Father, I'm going to give you what you want. I'm letting you go."

As if he's been waiting for those exact words, the tension in his body eases. "Thank you, son."

I glance at my man. "Ruslan, will you take him to the car?"

"Come on, Clive, I'll help you downstairs," Ruslan says.

The moment they disappear through the door, Rowan comes to stand beside me. "Will you tell Noah the truth?"

I shake my head. "He didn't want innocent blood on his hands. I won't stain them with my mistake."

"You're handing him over in exchange for Skye and her sister, aren't you?"

The answer comes without hesitation because it's what I decided to do even before Father's confession. I swore to protect her and failed. That won't happen again. "I'll give Gideon my soul if that's what he asks for."

22

ARRAN

"He won't show up if you're there," I tell Luca when he insists on coming to the address on the outskirts of Philadelphia that I was given. "You have to wait far enough away that he won't suspect you'll follow."

"But he has Sofia." He tightens his hold on my car door, his knuckles turning white.

"He also has Skye and her little sister."

"You're not likely to make it out of this alone," he argues. "Not if Gideon thinks you'll just take your father's place. You need backup."

I peer out at the road that leads to where I need to go. We're parked about a mile away. I'm in one of Luca's Tahoes, my father sitting beside me. Luca, Ruslan, and Rowan rode behind us. The plan is to have them wait here. Close, but not too close. If either Skye or any of Gideon's men come this way, they will act.

But there's a good chance we'll be taken to another facility altogether. And he's right. The chances of me making it out alive are slim to none. I'm not stupid enough to believe otherwise. As long as Skye and Maisie make it out, I don't give a fuck.

"If you don't hear from them in an hour, start the search." I tap the Maxton House ring on my finger. "Ruslan will be able to track the chip in it."

Luca nods and pushes away from the truck. "Good luck."

I turn to Father. "Are you ready?"

He shuts his eyes and sighs as if in relief. "Yes."

Five minutes later, we arrive at a nondescript warehouse that any passerby might assume is abandoned. But I can see the technology being used as a clear indication that although the physical space might be empty, it is by no means abandoned.

I stop the vehicle in the back as instructed and wait.

"Is he coming?" Father anxiously scans the area.

"Yes," I reply, spotting the three SUVs caravanning our way.

They cage us in, then several armed men spill from them, their guns pointed toward us.

"Out with your hands up," someone orders.

We do as we're told, placing our hands behind our heads. One of the men rushes toward me, pushing me onto my knees on the ground. After binding my wrists at my back with rope, he pats my suit, checking the pockets and my back for any weapons. When he finds my phone, he tosses it onto the pavement and crushes it with his boot.

On the other side of the Tahoe, I can hear my father going through the same thing.

"Clear!" both guards yell.

We're hauled to our feet and tossed into the back of one of their vehicles. Within a matter of seconds, we leave the warehouse behind.

I say nothing. Simply stare out at the road ahead as I quietly work the Maxton House ring off my finger, and jam it into the crook of the seat. It is now up to Ruslan to find us.

———

Although it shouldn't surprise me to be taken to my old family home, it does. Or perhaps it's not so much surprise as it is shock to once again be in the place where Kate was murdered.

From my position on my knees beside Father in the front parlor, I can clearly see beyond the dining room toward the kitchen.

I'd assume it was just a coincidence that we've been placed here to wait for our sentence to be carried out, but I doubt anything Gideon does is accidental. He wants us to have a good view of the murder scene. An added bonus, if you will, to his revenge.

I turn to my father. He's lowered his head, choosing to stare at the floor instead. Tears roll down his cheeks, landing softly on the expensive carpet that will soon be covered in his blood. Possibly mine too.

"Good afternoon." Gideon strolls into the room, followed closely by a blonde woman I assume is Scarlet.

Behind them, two huge guys escort Skye and Maisie, each holding one of them. Another goon comes in with two duffel bags and sets them near the entrance.

Skye looks up and my eyes meet hers, and when I see the terror in them, I try to stand.

"I wouldn't if I were you," Gideon says as I'm shoved back down hard by his henchwoman.

"You have us," I hiss. "Let them go."

"But that wasn't the deal."

"Then what is it?" I demand.

He lifts his gaze to Skye and grins evilly. "I'd like *her* to tell you."

She shakes her head. "No."

"Skye. I'm not asking again. Tell him our deal. What is your ticket to freedom?"

Trembling, she utters, "A bullet in Clive's head."

"And who must put it there?"

Her breathing accelerates to the point I believe she'll hyperventilate. "Me."

Although her sister begins to quietly sob, I don't take my gaze off her. She's afraid but desperately doing her best to remain strong. Fighting to keep her composure.

Gideon stands between us, forcing my attention back to him. "Your lovely Skye puts a bullet between Clive's eyes, then they can grab those bags with their belongings and leave."

"Why have her do it?" I ask, my tone even and unaffected. "I won't blame her for it."

He tilts his head and narrows his gaze. "Won't you? Not even a little bit?"

"Just get it done with." Father, who until now has remained quiet, says.

His grin vanishing, Gideon moves around him. "Just get it over with," he repeats. "Did my father use those same words when you and the others executed him? Oh, that's right." He pauses, lifting his forefinger as if he's just realized something. "My father wasn't even given the chance to beg. He was gagged and riddled with bullets before he was tossed into the river."

"Stephen deserved to die for the things he did," Father says, surprising me. "As do I. So. Just. Do. It."

"Not even a hint of remorse. You killed him because he figured out a way to gain power, and you envied him." Gideon tuts.

"Is that what you believe?" Father asks, more lucid now than I've seen him in a long time. "No wonder you're so angry."

Gideon cocks his head. "If that's a lie, enlighten me."

Father stares at him. "It isn't a lie. But it isn't exactly true either, is it?"

"For fuck's sake, don't speak in riddles," Gideon snaps. "What the fuck is that supposed to mean?"

"Nothing." Father replies, turning from him.

Gideon observes my father for a long while, as if he's trying to read him, his jaw working furiously. Then he nods at Skye. "Do it."

Skye is released and pushed toward us. Scarlet grabs her hand and places a gun in it.

"Don't do it, Skye," Maisie cries. "Please. Please don't make her do it."

Scarlet gives her a quick glance but turns away from her. She grabs Skye by the shoulders and pushes her until she's positioned in front of my father. Wrapping her fingers around her wrist, she forces her to lift the gun.

A sob escapes Skye, but she swallows it down. "Don't make me do this."

"There is one bullet. You either put it in Clive's head, or Scarlet will put it in your sister's," Gideon grits through his teeth. "You choose."

Scarlet turns a hard glare at her boss before she tells Skye, "Don't make me kill Maisie."

"Are you watching, Arran?" Gideon asks. "Watch."

"Please don't!" Maisie screams.

"Look away, Maze," Skye tells her.

My gut clenches and bile rises in my throat. Every cell in my body wants to react, to throw myself onto my father and protect him. The only thing that stops me is standing in front of me, her gray eyes locked on mine. If I do anything, it will be *she* who dies.

Gideon has played this game very well. He's cornered us all. Cornered us all to the point we can't do anything but follow his rules. And even when we do, in the end, we're all going to lose.

"Do it!" Gideon commands, his patience waning.

"No. No!" Maisie continues.

Skye shifts her attention to my father.

"I forgive you, child," he says.

The gun begins to shake so violently in Skye's grasp, I fear she might lose it.

"Fuck this shit." Scarlet snatches the weapon from Skye and, in one swift move, shoots.

Blood spatters the side of my face and I suck in a breath. Horror fills me as I watch my father slump to the floor.

"Father!" I call to him, knowing it's pointless but unable to help myself.

In the distance, I hear Maisie screaming. I turn to her numbly. Watch as she manages to free herself from the man and runs through the front door.

"Maisie!" Skye tries to follow, but she's stopped when one of the men clamps onto her shoulder and pulls her back.

Scarlet hisses something at Gideon and disappears after Maisie.

Gideon stares after them for a moment. Then he looks down at the body of my father. His expression is impassive. Disgusted. "Even dead, they don't bring me peace."

"That's because revenge rarely does," Skye sneers.

"You're killing people for nothing."

He turns his steel-blue eyes on her and, though I'm sure it's hard not to, she doesn't shrink away from him. My brave girl.

"What would you know of revenge?" Gideon asks in a strained tone. "Have you ever tasted it?"

"No. But I don't need to to know it's not as sweet as they say. All it does is leave you hungry for more. You're living proof."

He smiles that fucking smile I can't stand. "Ah, but it is. In fact, I'm going to give you a little taste right now."

Almost hazed, I see him take out a firearm from his back pocket and point it toward me. He pulls back on the hammer and places his fingertip on the trigger.

Before he has a chance to lift it to my head, Skye tears away from the man holding her and is on Gideon like a wild thing. She's kicking him and smacking him, screaming at him to leave us alone.

He manages to fling her off. But before he can aim the gun my way again, she's standing in front of me, her arms spread out protectively. "You're done here, Gideon. You got what you came for. You fucked with us all. Now go."

"Get out of the fucking way," he demands.

Fear like I've never felt before grips me at the thought that he might hurt her too. "Skye, what are you doing? Move!" I attempt to push her with my shoulder, but it's hard to do bound the way I am.

"Move, Skye," he says.

"No!"

Gideon stares at her intensely, holding the firearm threateningly at her. But he doesn't shoot. Simply remains still, eyes locked on hers.

He hesitates long enough that Scarlet returns. "Luca

and his men are pulling down the street. Maisie's headed toward them. We need to go."

"How the fuck do they know where we are?" He looks at me, and I shrug. Growling, he shoves the gun back into his hip holster. Then to me, he says, "Keep your head down and you'll live. Take Clive's place, and you'll end up buried beside him."

With that, Gideon and his men retreat out the back.

Skye turns to me. "Are you hurt?"

"It wouldn't matter if I was."

She comes behind me and works to undo the rope at my wrists. All the while, I observe my father's chest, watching for any sign that he might be breathing. Praying for that rise and fall to tell me he's still alive.

But when Skye frees me, and I go to him, his body is already cooler than it should be. I feel for a pulse, but there is none. The once great Clive Maxton, the man who taught me everything I know, is dead.

The pain that's been threatening to choke me since the decision was made to turn ourselves over to Gideon doesn't get worse like I thought it would. Instead, I'm left hollow and numb.

I take Father's hand and close my eyes, wishing I was in better standing with God so that I could pray for his soul. But I do it anyway because that's what he wanted more than anything. Peace and forgiveness.

Skye kneels beside me. "I don't even know what to say. Everything seems wrong."

The front door opens and I whirl, defensively pushing Skye behind me. But when I see Luca and Ruslan enter, I relax.

"We tracked your ring," Ruslan says.

"Where is Gideon?" Luca asks.

"He did what he came to do and left," I reply.

Luca peers over my shoulder and does the sign of the cross over his chest. "May he rest in peace."

Ruslan takes his leather jacket off and places it over my father. "He will be missed."

"Your sister is with Gunn," Luca tells Skye. "But you should probably go talk to her."

Skye nods. She looks at me one more time, her gaze sad, before picking up her bag and heading outside.

"What do you want to do?" Luca asks. "I can have the scene cleaned."

"There's no point. People are already asking where Clive Maxton has disappeared to." Besides, he deserves a proper burial. Not one done hastily in an unnamed tomb.

"The police must be called in, then," Ruslan says.

"There will be questions," Luca adds. "They're going to put you through the wringer."

"I have a good lawyer."

Ruslan takes out his phone. "I'll get in touch with the police chief. Keep this as discreet as possible."

As he does that, I go to stand by the window. Skye is speaking with Gunn outside the Tahoe. Inside, Maisie is sitting almost catatonically. It's going to be a long time before either of them get over this. Before I do.

"Will you keep them at Briar House until I can sort this out?" I ask Luca.

"Of course."

"You'll keep them safe?"

Luca nods in determined affirmation. "You're part of the alliance now. We protect our own."

I don't tell him that Skye isn't one of us because she's not mine anymore. I don't tell him, because in my mind, she always will be.

23

SKYE

It takes two days for Arran to sort out things back in Philly. He hasn't called me once. Though I'm not sure I would talk to him if he did.

Carina has kept me updated on everything. He was obviously detained for questioning after Clive's death. But things were quickly wrapped up when it was determined he'd also been a victim. Either way, the case will be open for a while. Now it's just a matter of cleaning up the mess left behind.

What a mess it is too.

Never has my life made less sense than it does now. Never has it been so difficult to find my place.

While Carina and Luca have welcomed us into their home for as long as we need, both Maisie and I have had a hard time acclimating.

Maisie has yet to snap out of that strange state where she's retreated into herself and spends most of her time locked up in the room assigned to her. I've tried several times to talk to her about everything that happened, but she just smiles and puts on her earphones, shutting me out.

I'm left to wonder how deep her new wounds run. Was it seeing Clive shot that traumatized her? Or was it the fact that the woman she'd put on a pedestal did the shooting? The new hero, who proved to be nothing but a villain.

Those thoughts swim through my mind on constant repeat while, at the same time, I'm reeling from my own experience. But unlike Maisie, I don't stay holed up in the room I was given. I can hardly stand being in it, not when it's the same one Arran and I shared.

Arran.

I am so utterly torn about everything that has to do with him, it feels like I'm physically being ripped apart.

Even after all he did, I want to go back in time and spare him the pain of losing his father the way he did.

He turned him in. For me. He watched him die. For me. And I love him all the more for it.

But he wouldn't have had to if he hadn't killed my father, a thing for which I'll hate him until the day I die.

How does a person live this way? Can such intense love and unadulterated hate reside in the same heart? Will they war inside me until I go mad from it? Or will one eventually win over the other? Which is stronger, love or hate?

I tear at my hair and move away from the dining room window I've been staring out of for over an hour.

"Hey," Carina says from the doorway. "You okay?"

Shrugging, I say on a sob, "No."

"If you want to talk, I'm here."

"I think it's time for us to go." I sigh. "We need to start fresh. Somewhere quiet, where we can reset."

She folds her arms over her chest and leans against the doorjamb. "Where would you go?"

"Vermont. My father set up a place for us there."

She nods. "You can take one of the cars if you'd like."

"I'd appreciate that." Secretly, I'd hoped she'd offer it. It will certainly save me the hassle of a rental.

There's a knock at the front door, and from the sound of it, Luca answers. A few moments later, he appears at the dining room entrance.

"Someone's here to see you, Skye."

Arran steps in and I almost gasp at the sight of him in sweatpants and a T-shirt, his hair disheveled and at least two days of growth on his cheeks. His blue irises contrast harshly against the redness of his eyes and the dark circles beneath.

"We'll leave you two alone," Carina says, taking Luca by the hand and dragging him away.

"You look nice," Arran says, his gaze trailing over me. Although he seems to have seen better days, the heat is still there. It still touches me intimately.

I cross my arms, not willing to show my body's automatic response to him. "Thanks, so do you."

He laughs. "That's a lie."

"It is," I admit. "Are you getting sleep?"

"No." He takes a step closer to me. "I can't sleep without you."

I don't tell him I'm struggling too. That the bed feels like an abyss, cold and dark without him pressed against me. Instead, I say, "It's time for Maisie and me to go."

"I'd like you to stay longer."

"We can't."

"Please. I've been working hard to take care of the men who are after you, but it's a lot to figure out exactly who your father had dealings with. It will take weeks to sort out. I'm not asking you to come home with me, but at least stay here."

"I don't have that collar anymore, remember? I don't belong to you. You don't need to protect me," I snap.

He winces. "But I want to."

"No. Maisie and I will leave first thing in the morning for Vermont. We have a house there."

His lips thin when he realizes my mind is made up. "Do you have your cell phone on you?"

"Why?" I ask before I realize that, like a good girl, I'm already handing it to him. Fuck me.

He takes it and enters something. "I want you to have my number. Just in case."

"I won't call you, Arran. I never want to see you again."

Pausing from what he's doing, he lifts his eyes to mine. In them, there's something I've never seen before—an ache so deep, I instinctively want to reach out to him. To comfort him. But I don't.

I extend my hand and ask for my phone back. He places it in my palm, his fingers grazing my skin. They linger there, burning me. Making me want to scream because I can't move away.

Then, without warning, he drops to his knees, his head down. "Forgive me, Skye. Please. Please forgive me."

A cry escapes me, and I look away from him. "Forgive you the way you forgave my dad when you believed he was behind Kate's death?"

Shaking his head, he says, "I didn't know. I... I didn't know he was innocent. I would never have hurt an innocent man."

"You knew *I* was innocent, but you hurt me anyway!" I scream the last. "You mentally punished me every time you touched me. You made me hate myself for wanting you."

"I didn't touch you to hurt you, Skye! I touched you

because I *needed* to. Because from the moment I saw you, I wanted you."

"And you're not a man who will be denied," I hiss. "Well, I'm denying you now. You don't deserve me or my forgiveness."

Lifting his gaze, he says, "I don't deserve it. But I'm asking for it, nonetheless. I'm in love with you."

It's like a spear to the chest. An agony that can only come from hearing the words from the person I love beyond reason after discovering the true monster inside him.

"Shut up!" I cry out from the pain and stumble back as he reaches for me. "Don't touch me!"

"Skye."

I straighten my spine in spite of the fact that no man has ever hurt me this way. "Maisie and I are leaving. Do not follow us. If you love me the way you say you do, you will let me go. I never want to see you again."

"Skye, forgive me," he repeats, blinking up at me, seeming so lost and confused.

For a moment, it's like I'm abandoning a lost puppy. I hesitate, my broken heart yearning for him too. "I'm sorry, Arran. I just don't know how."

———

The house is just like I remember. It's been years since Daddy brought us to Vermont to visit the place he planned on buying with Momma. Only, she died before their dreams of a vacation spot on Lake Champlain ever came true.

With Harold Greene's help, he eventually bought it. It's listed under a completely different name, though. Someone who doesn't exist, because the people in it aren't supposed to exist either.

I tug the flannel blanket around my shoulders and sit on the swing facing the water. It's serene. Surrounded by nature and clean, cool air. Far from the overwhelming sounds of the city and its glaring lights. Far from danger and men who want me dead.

Far from Arran.

That sharp ache in my chest returns full force, and I swallow down the sob that's threatening to emerge. I refuse to let it go. There's no point.

But something distracts me. A bird or a squirrel moving in the trees that surround us, and I forget to hold it in. So the cry comes out, pained and incredibly sad even to my own ears.

"Fuck!" I wipe angrily at my tears. How is it that even though I'm in this wonderful place, safe and sound, the man still hurts me?

I hate him. I hate Arran for what he did to my father. And I hate him more for making me love him. I hate myself too because even though I shouldn't, I love him so much more than I hate him.

Misery loves company.

Turning away from the lovely sight of the lake, I peer through the French doors into the living room, where Maisie sleeps. I get up and go inside.

I sit on the floor beside the couch my sister is lying on and stare at her. Tears streak her cheeks too and sadness mars the space between her brows.

We arrived over a week ago in a Tahoe Carina gave us, and both of us are still feeling the effects of everything that happened. The things we left behind. The people.

At least she's sketching again. I take the pencil dangling from her fingers and place it on the table.

It wakes her, her lids opening slowly. She blinks a couple of times as she focuses on me. "You've been crying."

"A little."

"For Arran."

Unheeded, tears begin to flow again. "Ugh, why does this keep happening?" I wipe the sleeve of my shirt over my eyes.

"You miss him."

I shake my head, trying desperately to deny it. "How can I miss him after everything he's done? He's a bad man."

Maisie pushes herself into a sitting position and pats the spot beside her. I sit there and take her hand.

"He did something really bad," she says. "But he didn't know, right?"

I consider her question for a second. "No."

"I don't think he's a bad man."

"You think I should forgive him."

"Do you have a choice? You're so sad. We're both so sad. Is keeping him away worth it?" Her question shocks me. "I want to go home, Skye."

Pulling her toward me, I place my chin on her head. Tears roll from my eyes, landing on her hair. "This is our home now, Maze."

"Is that true? Or are you just saying it for my benefit?"

I wish it to be true, because I ache for home just as much as Maisie does. At least, that's what I say for *my* benefit.

But the truth is that when I shut my lids and think of that warm place I want to return to, it's not the house in Chestnut Hill I grew up in. It's not even the house on Delancey Street. It's the arms of the man I...

Abruptly, I straighten, wiping the wetness from my

cheeks. I cannot love him. I cannot love the monster who killed my father.

Needing to change the mood, I reach for Maisie's sketchbook. "Do you have anything new?"

"Not really."

I flip through the pages. Many of her drawings are ones I've seen before. Some I haven't.

But it's one that I *have* that gets my attention because something is different. She's changed the clothes of her character, making the shirt she wore into a turtleneck, adding a few knives and weapons. And the title. What once read *Rage* has been scratched out. Beneath it is a new one. *Scarlet*.

That's the source of my sister's sadness. This woman who was a part of her traumatic capture. Stockholm syndrome can take many shapes. In her case, she sees Scarlet as some hero.

"She's not Rage," I say, annoyed.

Maisie snatches the book. "I never said she was."

"But you believe it." I tuck a piece of her dark hair behind her ear. Softening my tone, I say, "She's not your character come to life, Maze."

She peers at the picture. "Except she is."

"No, she's not. You're too old to believe something like that."

"Skye, she's exactly the way I've drawn her. It's like..." As she searches for the word, her face lights up and I feel a pang of jealousy that she looks up to her so much. "It's like I wished her to come to me and she did. And if *she* did, then maybe..."

"Maybe what?"

"Maybe Momma can too." She flips the page and shows me *Justice Girl*, the character she based off our mother.

I stare at the familiar face, the one I see often in my dreams. "Is that what this is about? This obsession with Scarlet? You think Momma can come to life?"

My brows pinch as I observe the myriad of emotions that cross my sister's face. Hope. Excitement. A childlike need that breaks my heart.

"Maisie. Momma is never coming back. You know that."

She rears back as if I've slapped her, her eyes widening. Then she whirls away from me as she stands. "You don't understand anything."

"Maze, wait!" I call out, but she doesn't stop until she gets to her room and slams the door.

I remain like that, staring after her, feeling like a first-class idiot for not knowing how to mend her heart. But how could I when my own wounds are still bleeding?

Lying down, I tuck my knees into my chest and cry.

———

I must have been exhausted, not from any kind of physical activity, but mentally tired. The sort that comes from too much thinking. From continuous scenarios playing in my mind over and over again, a treadmill for my brain, moving and moving but going nowhere.

My mind shut down and I fell into the most restless sleep I've ever had. I woke constantly from nightmares where I lost Maisie, had conversations with Daddy where he asked how I could love the man who killed him, and falling. Lots of falling.

But every time I woke up, I went back to sleep so fast, I couldn't get off the couch. It was like being drugged almost, conscious enough to know it but unable to move.

By the time I'm finally able to sit up and shake off the haze of sleep, it's six in the morning.

I wipe my hands over my face and sigh, still so tired. Always so tired.

"Coffee. I need coffee." I push up and peer around the dark space, using my cell phone to illuminate my way to the kitchen.

There, I turn on the light and yawn, then drag my feet to the counter. Lazily, I start a pot. As it heats, I look around without really seeing, barely registering anything. That is, until I spot a note stuck on the white fridge by a little grape magnet.

Frowning, I grab it and read.

I'm sorry, Skye. This isn't home. It never will be. I'm going back.

Maisie

It's as if the world tilts on its axis. Everything seems to spin and I lose my balance, stumbling back against the wall. She's gone back home. Back to the danger.

Immediately, my mind goes to the men who are still hunting us because Gideon didn't fulfill his end of the bargain. And I think of her, so young and foolish.

How long has she been gone? How did she get there?

"Dammit!"

I grab my phone and dial her, but no answer. I dial again and again. Then I text.

Me: Where the hell are you?

Me: Please, I'm so worried.

Me: Why are you doing this?

Me: Maze, I swear to God, if you don't answer me, you're going to be in worse trouble!

Shoving my feet into my shoes, I go in search of my car keys. They're gone. I race to the door and peer out into the gravel drive to confirm that she has in fact taken the Tahoe. Just because she has her permit and could drive Daddy's small Mercedes, she thinks she can drive that giant all the way home?

"Fuck!" I throw the phone and scream.

Then I have to go dig it out of the bushes. With a shaking hand, I dial the first person who comes to mind in my desperation for help.

"Maxton," he answers.

"She's gone, Arran. She's gone!"

24

ARRAN

I'm a ghost, moving around aimlessly, barely there. A mere shadow of what I was before she came into my life.

If Luca thought I'd be any kind of help with the alliance, I believe he's been disappointed. Ruslan traced the Maxton House ring I took off in Gideon's vehicle to a junkyard. It appears Gideon suspected I'd done something to be so easily found back at my father's house, and he discovered it.

While I've still provided other assistance, the ring could have proven so much more useful in finding where Sofia is being kept.

But it's not the ring that's on my mind right now.

I tug the diamond collar from my pocket. I've been carrying it around with me, like some fucking memento of one of the biggest tragedies to happen to me.

"Why do you do that?" Skye asked me once, annoyed that I'd touched it.

"Because it's a symbol of what you are to me," I had replied.

It was the truth. This collar is a symbol, one that, at the time, I couldn't wrap my mind around because it defied the very strict laws that govern me.

I am in control.

I am ruler of my dominion.

I am Arran Maxton.

Above all, I am... Hers.

Fuck, I might as well have been wearing the damned thing myself. It would have been more appropriate.

Because it didn't matter what the contract said. It didn't matter that it was she who wore the collar. I was the one enslaved, my heart torn from my chest and offered to her on a silver platter. And I couldn't understand it!

How? How could that be when I believed her to be the daughter of my enemy? How could I be so willing to fall onto my knees and worship her, castrate my own brother, and even give up my father?

I did it. I'd do it all again. I'd fucking slit my own wrists if that's what she commanded, because I'm...hers.

But like a dog whose owner has abandoned him, I'm also left to wander. Roaming without aim. Without purpose. Just waiting for the next minute to pass and the next, wondering if she'll ever return to me.

"Will you pray with me today?" Father Nikolai asks, sitting beside me.

I look around, completely unsurprised to find myself in his church again, even though I don't remember driving here. "God won't hear a man like me."

"God hears us all." There is so much conviction in his words that I want to believe them.

But it's hard to do when the memories of the things I've done linger. The people I've killed, regardless of the reason.

The crimes against my own brother, even if he's deserved them. But it's the blood of one innocent man that truly condemns me.

Letting out a lengthy exhale, which seems to be all I do lately because it's hard to breathe with so much weight on my chest, I say, "Ruslan says the parish is doing well."

He smiles kindly, his old eyes crinkling. "Very well, thanks to him. And you, of course."

We both look forward, up to the large cross that hangs over the pulpit. I'm not sure what drew me to this place. Perhaps I'm hoping for some sort of redemption, if not from Skye, then from God.

"He does listen, child," Nikolai says, as if he can hear my thoughts.

"I don't know what to say to him."

"Perhaps you say nothing. Simply open yourself to him." He pats my shoulder and stands, leaving me to stare ahead.

I sigh yet again and close my eyes, clearing my thoughts. Opening myself as he said. For a moment, everything inside me is silent. Then when I do speak, I'm ashamed that the first thing I do is ask for something. And it's not forgiveness or even a prayer for my family. It's a wish for Skye.

My phone rings, and I tug it from my pocket.

"Maxton," I answer.

"She's gone, Arran. She's gone!"

I stand, my heart pounding in my chest. "Skye?"

"I'm sorry. I didn't know who else to call."

"Who's gone?"

"Maisie." I hear sniffling and a soft sob. "She went back home, Arran. She took the Tahoe. It will be hours before I can get there. What if she's already gotten there and someone was waiting?"

My mind races with all the worst possible scenarios. Things that could happen to a young girl. The horror of my sister's death and it happening again to her.

Thomas Cameron had many debts. But it's not the amount of money he owed that's the real danger. It's the people he owed it to.

When I told Skye it would take a while to sort it all out, I wasn't exaggerating. There are still many of those debts left unpaid. With them safely in Vermont, I didn't make it a priority the way I should have. I was taking my time.

Fuck!

"Where are you going, child?" Father Nikolai calls from the pulpit as I rush out of the church.

"There's an emergency. Pray for us," I yell over my shoulder. Then to Skye, I ask, "Do you have any idea if she's made it home yet?"

"No. She won't answer my calls. It's my fault, Arran. She begged me to go back, but I didn't want to. I was afraid."

"None of this is your fault," I tell her.

"Arran." She sniffles, and the fact that she's openly crying now after being so brave tears at my soul. "Can you get to her?"

I make a mental map, calculating the amount of time it will take to travel the distance. I'm not far from Chestnut Hill, but I know someone who might be closer.

"Can you get to the regional airport?" I ask.

"Yes."

"Go there. I'm going to make arrangements for you."

"What about Maisie?" A door slams and she's out of breath, as if she's running.

"I'll ask Gunn and Ruslan to head there now. They're in that area."

"Please hurry, Arran. Please save my sister."

With determination, I say, "I will."

25

MAISIE

Home sweet home.

Only, it's not as sweet as I imagined it would be. I thought I'd return to warm memories, the familiar scent. The feeling of safety I grew up with. Instead, I'm met with cold and eerie silence. It's dark too, as if even the early morning sunlight refuses to penetrate the lifelessness in here.

It never occurred to me that the power would be shut off. Or that when it was, any life left in the house would cease to exist. All that's left is a void where ghosts drift.

I sit on my bed and pull the blankets over my legs. When that doesn't work to dispel the chill that's crept over me, I rub my palms over my arms.

I've been here over an hour, and already, I want to call Skye and beg her to come pick me up. Regret fills me in a way it never has, and I'm so scared I'll never see the light again, I can hardly breathe.

Pulling my phone from my backpack, I almost do call her. But as I turn on the screen, I see something that changes my mind. Right below my sister's name in my contact list is Scarlet's.

She must have put her contact information in when I wasn't looking. But why would she do that?

Selecting it, I hit the Call button.

It rings only twice before she answers. "Maisie."

I stay quiet for a moment, until I muster up the courage to say, "You really *are* an assassin."

She blows out a breath. "I didn't want you to see that, kid. You shouldn't have seen it."

"It scared me," I admit.

"You'll never have to see Gideon or me ever again."

The house creaks, a noise it usually makes when the sun starts to heat the roof. I pick at some of the pilling on the old quilt that covers my bed. "Will you be okay?"

"Yeah. I'm always okay."

"Scarlet?"

"Hmm?"

"I— What the...?" There's another creak. Only, this time, it doesn't sound like the house warming up.

My brows pinch together as I listen more intently. There it is again but closer.

"Maisie, are you still there?"

As quietly as I can, I slip out of the bed. "I think there's someone in the house."

"What?"

"I came back to my old house. I think someone's in here."

"What? Fuck!" There's some thumping on the other end of the line that almost matches the racing of my heart as I move toward the door. "Maisie, where's your sister?"

"Vermont." The word comes out so low, I'm not sure if she can hear me.

"Shit. Fuck!"

I peer out of my bedroom, barely poking my head through the doorway. Another thump downstairs has me tucking back in fast.

"Listen to me, Maisie," Scarlet says. "Are you near an exit?"

My eyes flick to the window. I could jump. But it's a straight drop to the ground. Not even a dang bush to break my fall. If I land the wrong way, I'm dead. I'm an artist, not a stunt girl. My dad's room, however, has a window right over the porch. "Across the hall."

"Do you still have the knife I gave you?"

Looking at my bag on the bed, I nod as if she can see me. "I don't know if I can use it."

"Hopefully, you won't have to." She slams a door, then I hear the revving of an engine. "I'm less than five minutes from Chestnut Hill. Three minutes tops. Can you find your way there?"

I swallow down hard, my legs trembling. "Yes."

"Get your knife and get out of the house. If the mother-fucker gets to you, slash him, and don't stop until he's dead. I'll be there as soon as I can." She hangs up and the sudden lack of sound has me shaking worse.

Tucking the phone into the back of my jeans, I tiptoe to the bed and dig out the small knife she gifted me after I was able to cut her with it. Said I earned it.

But it's one thing to fight an opponent you know isn't trying to kill you and another to go against an intruder who most certainly is. Because anyone sneaking into my house can't be up to anything good.

I plaster myself to the wall and listen. The stairs are wooden and noisy, something I complained about on the rare occasion I snuck out. I'm not complaining now.

When I don't hear anything, I risk stepping out of my room. Slowly, my eyes glued to the stairwell, I make my way around.

The dragging of an object, maybe one of the chairs that flank the table in the foyer, has me ducking into Skye's room. My lungs burn as I try desperately to control my breathing, the knife held tightly to my chest.

Whoever is down there—and now there's no doubt in my mind that someone is—coughs. A door is opened, followed by the sound of a low male voice. "Power's out."

"Johnny said he saw a flashlight," says a second voice and I have to stifle a gasp.

There are two men down there. Everything Scarlet taught me this past week may help me, and that's a huge *may*, against one man. But two?

"We need to clear the house," the second man says. "Make sure the bitch hasn't returned."

"I'll finish down here. You go up."

I sink further into the room, carefully placing one foot behind the other. The stairs begin to creak and groan as the man ascends.

My heart climbs into my throat as I enter the Jack and Jill bathroom Skye and I shared. It's all I can think to do that won't have me cornered, a freaking sitting duck waiting to be slaughtered.

He's upstairs now. It might be my overactive imagination, but I can almost hear him breathing.

Tears well up in my eyes, and I hate that I'm such a chicken right now. All the action movies I ever starred in in my head, all the different comic characters I created and saw myself as, and I can barely keep myself from crying.

But it's not a matter of being brave or scared. I either sit here and do nothing, or I fight like hell.

His steps round the corner, and I back up into my room again, pointy end of the blade up and ready for when the jerk appears.

However, the attack doesn't come from the front like I expect it to. It's from behind, and I never stood a chance.

A hand wraps around my wrist as another covers my mouth. I'm about to scream but am silenced by the voice in my ear.

"Shh. It's me. Scarlet." She pulls me back slightly, then releases me. When I turn to look at her, relief flooding me so fast I swear I'm going to pass out, she places a finger to her lips.

I nod. Then she mimes, telling me there's one man in my room but three downstairs.

My eyes bulge as I realize how much trouble I was really in.

She indicates for me to follow, and I go into the bathroom with her. When she presses herself against the wall beside the door that leads into Skye's bedroom, she lifts her hand, and I stop beside her.

That's when I notice the knife she's carrying. It's so big, it makes mine look like a toy. She holds it loosely in her right palm. Then, taking a deep breath, she glides into the room.

I'm not sure if the man sees her coming. There are a few thumps and a sickening gurgling that makes me nauseous just to imagine. I already have the memory of one death in my mind, and it will never go away. Because I don't need another, I don't peek. I wait where Scarlet told me to until she appears, her knife dripping crimson liquid on the floor.

Again, she motions for me to follow. I remain close to her, my only shield against the remaining men.

We step out into the hall and are about to head down

the stairs when one of the goons decides to come to us. Scarlet moves us out of view so that he's not aware of the danger until it's too late.

Before I can shut my eyes, she attacks. It's so fast, so fascinating, I'm not sure I would have looked away if I could. She grabs him by one arm at the same time that she whirls, her blade slashing through the air. Two quick hits, one to the crook of his neck and shoulder, the other to his back, and it's over. He slumps forward, eyes unseeing. She catches him and helps him land softly.

Tilting her head, she listens intently for a moment, as if pinpointing the location of the others. She motions for me to stay put, then descends the stairs. But I've never been accused of being a good listener, especially not when I'm interested in something. And I'm very interested in not being left alone.

So I go down too, in time to watch her dispatch another guy. This one screams before she slits his throat, alerting the last goon to our presence. Unfortunately for me, I'm the first one he sees.

He lunges for me and I jump up so many stairs, I nearly make it all the way to the second floor again. But Scarlet manages to grab him by the ankles and drags him down to her level to take him out.

Breathing hard, she looks at me. Blood drips from her knife and her hair. I'm sure there's more of it smattering her tight black turtleneck and pants, but it's harder to see.

She looks like an avenger. A deadly weapon who saved me.

"You *are* Rage," I whisper. It doesn't matter what Skye says. Rage and Scarlet are the same.

"Kid, I—" She whirls just as another man, this one much bigger and meaner-looking than the others, attacks.

She blocks his punch, swinging her blade at him. But he easily avoids being gutted and smacks her across the face. Before I can even gasp at that, she kicks him two times consecutively, once in his leg and the other in his ribs.

They separate and stare at each other, smiling. Only then do I realize that the guy is one of Arran's friends. Gun, I believe he called him.

"Didn't think I'd have the chance to play with you again," he tells her, his grin wide.

"I thought we were dancing?" she returns his smile.

She drives forward. He jumps back, but she adjusts and manages to nick his arm.

When he touches the spot and brings back blood on his fingers, his grin widens. "Has your knife gotten bigger, or are you just happy to see me?"

Laughter bursts from her. "I like your smile... What was your name again?"

"Gunn. Two *n*'s."

"All right, Gunn with two *n*'s. When I take you down, I promise to carve that smile permanently on your face so that when you're lying in your coffin, everyone can still see those dimples."

"There are other ways you could kill me and leave me with a smile," he retorts.

"In your dreams."

"You already did, sweetheart. Many times over."

I frown, confused by their exchange. "Do you guys know each other?"

They both look at me as if they're surprised I'm there. Like I disappeared for a moment while they were having their weird exchange.

"She's one of the bad guys," Gunn says.

"So is he."

I glance between the two, who are still in battle stance, knives out, ready to fight. Something tells me they've fought before. And if they have and they're both standing here alive, they're equally matched.

Gunn grabs my arm and moves me behind him protectively. "Backup is on its way. You're safe now."

Backup? I look at Scarlet. She's an amazing fighter. Maybe better than Gunn. But how many men are coming? *Who* is coming? Would she end up killing people who are here to save me before dying herself?

I can't allow that.

I jump as high as I can and wrap my arms around Gunn's neck, making him stumble back.

"Scarlet, run!" I scream to her. Gunn tries to dislodge me, but I hold on like my life depends on it.

Scarlet's lips thin as she hesitates, and for a moment, I think she might still try to fight him. Just as she seems to change her mind and whirl around, Arran appears behind her looking all beat up, as if he's taken on a man or two himself.

"Watch out!" I yell. But it's too late.

She doubles over as he thrusts something into her gut. Though she only remains paralyzed for a split second, it feels like an eternity. Or maybe it's that everything goes in slow motion. His hand slicing through the air, hitting her, then moving back out. The small black blade he's holding is dripping blood, her blood, on the floor.

"Scarlet!" I drop from Gunn's back and try to go to her, but he grabs me before I can get a step in.

Now everything speeds up. Scarlet falls against the wall, holding her side, gasping. But she's as alert as ever, her green eyes darting from spot to spot.

Arran nears her again, probably wanting to finish her

off. A mistake on his part, because, injured or not, she's still able to kick ass. And that's exactly what she does.

She swings one of her legs, knocking him off his feet. When he attempts to get up, she kicks him in the face.

Without waiting for him to recover, she runs in the opposite direction and disappears from sight. Gunn tosses me like a rag doll onto Arran and chases after her.

Arran stands and extends his hand to me. I slap it away. "You stabbed her!"

He seems taken aback. "She was trying to hurt you."

"No she wasn't. She's my friend!"

Gunn returns, wiping sweat and blood from his brow. "Kid, that woman there is no one's friend. She's a hellcat."

"Did Arran kill her?" I demand.

He purses his lips. "Did you not hear me say she's a hellcat? They have like a thousand lives. It would take more than a little knife to do the trick."

Arran grumbles something under his breath as he tucks the knife away. Then he comes to stand in front of me. "Skye called. She was afraid something would happen to you."

Some of my anger fades when I hear the humble tone in his voice. "She called you?"

"Yes. But I wasn't close enough. Gunn was."

I turn to the big guy. "Sorry Scarlet got you in the head."

"You mean this?" He points to the nasty scratch over his temple. "That was all you, kid."

"Oh." I grimace. "Sorry."

Gunn peers out the window. "Looks like the cavalry is here."

When I turn back to Arran, he's on the phone. "We have her," he says, looking at me. "She'll be okay. I swear it."

"Is that Skye?"

He nods as he continues to speak with Skye. "Go to Briar House instead and wait there. I'll bring her to you." Though I can't make out what she's saying on the other end, I can tell she's crying. "I know," Arran says. "I know. Me too. Let's talk when we get there."

"Where is she?" I ask him when he hangs up.

"Still on her way. But she'll be in New York soon."

"I messed up, didn't I?" I ask, suddenly filled with embarrassment.

He reaches for me and squeezes my shoulder. "No, Maisie. I'm the one who fucked up. But I promise to do everything in my power to make it right."

26

SKYE

I'm pacing the foyer like a caged lion, cracking my fingers, tugging my hair.

"She's all right, Skye," Emily says from the stairway, where she's sitting, watching me. "You don't have to worry anymore."

"I'll always worry. She's my little sister," I say. "I won't believe it until she's in front of me."

Carina stands abruptly. "Excuse me."

"Carina. Shit!" Emily reaches for her.

"It's okay. I'll be back."

Emily meets my puzzled gaze. "Her sister was killed recently."

I pause. "She didn't tell me she had a sister."

"A twin. Her name was Alma."

"How did she die?" I ask.

It takes her a moment to reply, and when she does, a chill goes up and down my spine. "Gideon's minion killed her. Scarlet."

My hand flies to my lips. "Oh my God. That's who Maisie stayed with."

"I know. That's why Carina wants to take Gideon and Scarlet out."

"She knew I was going to see Gideon. That could have been her chance."

Emily shrugs. "Your sister was more important at the time. She didn't want you to go through the same pain."

"I feel sick." I sit on the step beside Emily and tuck my head between my knees.

She rubs my back. "It's over now, though. Maisie is safe."

Now she is. But to think of how close she came. To think about the chance Carina gave up.

Just then, the front door opens. Luca walks in, followed closely by Maisie. Relief at seeing her standing there alive washes over me and I run to embrace her.

Tears flow freely as I hold her tightly, laughing and crying at the same time. "You had me so scared."

She buries her face in my chest and sniffles. "I'm sorry. I just... I wanted to come home."

"I know. And I'm sorry I didn't make sure you had one. I'm so sorry, Maze. But please promise you'll never scare me like that again."

Pulling away slightly, she peers up at me. "I promise."

I spot Arran behind her. He's looking worse for the wear, with a bruised cheek and a swelling eye.

Something inside me breaks. As if a wrecking ball has just slammed against the restraining wall that's been holding all of my doubt and hatred and fears, releasing them all at once. So I go to him and fling myself in his arms and cry into his chest.

We hold on tightly to each other. I think we're both too afraid to let go. When I lift my gaze to his, I see the hope in it. "Does this mean you forgive me?"

"I don't have a choice," I say, repeating what Maisie told me. "When I thought my world would fall apart, you were the first person I called out to. You were the one I trusted with Maisie's life."

"He kicked some ass," Maisie throws in. "Before Scarlet kicked his."

"Scarlet was there?" I frown.

"She saved me," Maisie says.

"Ismael Lopez's men were there," Gunn says. "That's who attacked."

"The important thing is that Maisie is safe. And we will deal with Ismael," Arran says. With his hands on my hips, his gaze lowered, he says, "But I need to know. Do you forgive me?"

I cup his rough cheek, trail my eyes over his tortured features, and I realize that it hurts me to see him like this. That I'd do anything to smooth the furrow between his brows and ease the tension in his jaw so that he smiles again.

Because I love him.

Letting out a long breath, one of many more to come, I let my heart do the talking. "Yes. I still want to kill you. But I might die without you. So I have no choice."

———

"Are you sure about this?" I ask when, a few days later, we walk into the five-bedroom house in Chestnut Hill, only a block away from my old home. Arran bought the place and paid an insane amount of money to have it vacated quickly so that we could move in and start our new lives together.

"It's going to be well guarded. Maisie will be able to see

her old friends and attend her school again. Things will never be the same, but it will be good for her."

My sister walks in behind us, looks around the place, and nods. "It'll do," she says.

"Where are you going?" I ask when she begins up the stairs.

"I'm going to stake my claim 'cause I have a feeling someone will take the best room if I don't."

I sigh. "Knowing her, she's probably going to take over the master bedroom."

"Let her." Arran grazes my cheek with the back of his fingers. "As long as you're in my bed, I don't care where it is."

Wrapping my arms around his waist, I lean into him. "Thank you, Arran. You didn't have to do all this."

"I did. I made promises to your father."

My brows pinch together. "What?"

"I went to church the other day. While I was there, I promised that if you came back to me, I'd take care of you forever. That I'd make sure Maisie had a family. That I'd give you two the home I robbed you of. That I'd love you more with each passing day."

"That's a lot to promise."

"Actually, that's only the tip of the iceberg." A smile curves his lips. Then he bends his head as if he's going to kiss me, but I pull back.

Grinning, I say, "Only do that if you mean it, Arran. You might not have a collar, but if you kiss me, you'll belong to me."

"Didn't you know? I've belonged to you all along. And I'll be yours always."

With those last words, he presses his lips to mine,

emblazoning his name on the contract that will bind us forever.

EPILOGUE
ROWAN

"That motherfucker Gideon Black is fuckin' with our shipments again," Axle tells me, tossing the newspaper on the desk in front of me. He points hard at the article that shows the accident which destroyed three of our trucks.

"You're sure it was him?" I ask unperturbed, my fingers steepled beneath my chin.

Axle bristles. "Who the fuck else would it be? He's makin' sure we can't fulfill our orders. We'll lose power before we even get it."

"We have power, Ax. But so does he. And money." I take the folded newspaper that's so worn, I can see the stress he's been under. And who the hell actually reads the paper anymore?

I peer at the photograph of the trucks that carried the coke from Mexico. They're still there. The three million dollars' worth of blow is not.

"If this were Gideon's handiwork, he would have burned it all. Whoever took this is just a thief."

"Then who?"

"The question we should be asking ourselves is, who would be able to sell that much without being caught?" It annoys me that anyone would have the balls to take what belongs to me. I also admire that type of gutsiness. "When is the next load coming in?"

"Three days."

"Up security. I want it tripled. We'll talk again this afternoon," I reply as I open my laptop and I begin to scroll through e-mails, ready to start the day.

"Will do, boss." Axle gets up and grabs his paper, chuckling as if relieved. "I was sure you'd be more pissed off than that after the news this morning."

I pause and glance up. "What news?"

His laughter dies on his lips and he swallows. "You know, the news. About Lou."

My heart nearly comes to a standstill at the sound of her name. "What about her?"

"There's a wedding announcement. In the paper."

I extend my hand and he shakily gives it back to me. The first thing I see when I unfold it is a photograph of the woman I almost married five years ago. She's in the arms of some rich douchebag who thinks he's a gangster because he occasionally gambles illegally.

The nuptials of Peter Deacon from Martha's Vineyard and Louisa Duran of Boston, to be celebrated this evening at Saint Mary's...

The paper crumples in my hands. My vision goes red as blood.

"Boss," Axle whispers.

"Get the men rounded up. We have a wedding to attend."

"Yes, sir."

When he walks out, I turn to peer out the window, my

hand tight on the hilt of the gun at my waist. If Lou thinks she's going to marry another man after she gave herself to me, she is sorely mistaken.

————

Dear Reader,

Thank you so much for reading Cruel Prince. I hope you enjoyed Arran and Skye's story. But the Sinacore Saga is far from over and the Ferryman still has lots of trouble up his sleeve!

Stay tuned for Rowan and Louisa's story, in Vicious Captor! Now available for pre-order.

Want to sink your teeth into another steamy and dark mafia series? Read The King of Bourbon Street, the first of the Mafia's Throne series out now!

The enemy sent a spy to bring me down, so I made her _MINE_.

I was born to rule, made by my father into the ruthless king of the Marcone crime family. My seat, a throne made of leather and gunpowder, forged by blood.

Now, a new threat has come to challenge my position, testing me for weakness by sending me the lovely Irish spy. Her sweet scent is a lure, her green eyes a weapon meant to seduce me until I lower my guard. And the secrets she holds the final blow meant to bring me to my knees.

I will let her in my home, and in my bed. And once she's there, she'll be under my rule.

Because I'm Enzo Marcone, and I am the King of Bourbon Street.

Aidèe Jaimes is a Mexican American, USA Today Bestselling author of dangerously addictive dark and contemporary romance. For more information on her novels and future releases, go to www.aideejaimes.com, or her Facebook hang with her in her Facebook group, Aidèe's Criminals.

OTHER BOOKS BY AIDÈE JAIMES

Merciless Vows (The Seven Deadly Sinacores, Book 1)
Ruthless Heir (The Seven Deadly Sinacores, Book 2)
Cruel Prince (The Seven Deadly Sinacores, Book 3)
Vicious Captor (The Seven Deadly Sinacores, Book 4)
Coming soon!
Devil's Den (A Diablos Cartel Prequel)
Play Me Darkly (A Diablos Cartel Standalone)
Wicked Obsession (Obsessed Duet, Book 1)
Needful Surrender (Obsessed Duet, Book 2)
King of Bourbon Street (Mafia's Throne, Book 1)
Queen of Deceit (Mafia's Throne, Book 2)
Reckless Prince (Mafia's Throne, Book 3)
Lawless Ruler (Mafia's Throne, Book 4)
Cruel Seduction (Cruel Duet, Book 1)
Ruthless Embrace (Cruel Duet, Book 2)
Private Investigation (Private Investigation Duet, Book 1)
Public Affair (Private Investigation Duet, Book 2)
The Professional (A World of Ember Novel)
The Ticket (The Affair, Book 1)

The Red Dress (The Affair, Book 2)
The Other Side (The Affair, Book 3)
The Promise (The Affair, Book 4)
Good Mr. King
Work Me

Made in the USA
Columbia, SC
21 October 2023

24758050R00157